Dedication

To my mom for always believing in me, and for being one of my best friends.

To my dad for always being there for me, and for having the best sense of humor.

To the greatest parents a girl could ask for! [Including my other dad, raising kiddos you didn't have to but did anyway.]

To my goofy, amazing siblings, each of you deserve the world and more.

To all those who love *'Erik the Phantom'* from *The Phantom of The Opera!* [There's a special scene just for you! ;)]

Huge thank you to all of my Kickstarter backers for helping this book come to life.

The following people not only backed my Kickstarter, but supported my dream of being an author! In no particular order:

1. Douglas Cline
2. Eric Peterson
3. Becky Sanders
4. Krista
5. Valerie Polhemus
6. Lori Ebel
7. Ryan Smith
8. Julie Jennings
9. Tammy Farrell
10. Kialy Giesking
11. Joesph Taylor
12. Gerald Alston
13. Andrew Grabenbauer
14. Rin Takeshima

Chapter One
One day until Sage's 25th Birthday

"Sage! Come on!" my friend, Clara says pulling on my arm, forcing me to walk with her into a house I don't recognize. I groan. Her middle length dirty blonde hair blows in the wind. Her green eyes look over to meet my blue ones. I'm 5'7, and she's shorter than me at 5'5.

"Whose house is this?" I ask looking around the exterior of the house. I look around at all the decor. It's decked out in halloween decorations. Skeletons, cobwebs, spiders, a giant reaper that leans forward and backwards to scare you, the works. The siding of the house is green, and has fake cobwebs on every window.

"It's Millie's cousin's house, stop worrying already. It's the night before your birthday and Halloween, let loose girl. We aren't getting any younger." I roll my eyes at her. Millie is her long-term girlfriend. They've been together since high school, and I'm honestly shocked that one of them hasn't popped the question yet. They are literally the definition of a perfect couple.

"But aren't we getting a little old for house parties like this?"

"Hell no." She looks at me like I've gotta be joking. She drags me into the house after the reaper animatronic does a hilarious number on her. She slaps my arm. "That was not funny."

"That was hilarious, and your reaction was priceless." I laugh, Millie finds us through the crowd and gives me a hug before kissing her girlfriend. I tell Millie about what happened and she agrees that it sounds hilarious.

"I'm sad I missed that!" Millie whines.

"We can try to recreate it," I offer, hooking my thumb towards the door.

"Fuck that, I need a drink now." Clara pushes through the crowd towards the kitchen, her wings attached to the back of her blue and purple fairy costume hit a few people in the head or faces earning her dirty looks. Of course she doesn't notice them, nor does she apologize. I laugh, following her and apologizing to the people for her.

"Seriously, Clara, you gotta apologize to people when you hit them." I laugh, as she glares at me.

"Just tell them I'm wasted." She offers.

"They probably just saw you walk in."

"I could have come from a different party." She says, rolling her eyes. I nod in agreement. She chugs three drinks back to back.

"Slow down a little," I laugh, she burps in my face in response. Gross, but thankfully I'm used to this after over ten years of friendship. I grab an alcoholic limeade from the ice bucket. I sip it as I watch people dance to the music.

This is kinda lame to do as an almost twenty-five year old. A lot of people from our high school graduating class are married with kids and here we are, still partying like we did in high school and college. We've been out of college for a year now. I honestly just want to be at home, in my bed with a book.

"Sage! Come in here with your Oracle cards!" Clara yells from the living room. I sigh, here we go. I hate doing readings at parties like this, with drunk people who get freaked out or think I talk to the dead. They are just cards, but they can tell you what you need to know. I walk into the living room, a group of people are sitting in front of a table with a spot on the other side of it open for me. I sit down across from them and pull out the only oracle deck I brought with me from my purse. Usually, I do readings with more than one deck at a time, but I wasn't going to carry a bunch with me to a random house.

"This is for entertainment purposes only. Take what resonates, leave what doesn't, no I don't talk to the dead. That's my little prep talk, so who's first?" Clara instantly raises her hand and repeats the word 'Me' until I tell her fine. The woman gets five readings a week from me if not more. I shuffle my cards and think about what she needs to know right now.

A few cards fly out as I shuffle, causing everyone watching to gasp. I put the deck down, and flip the cards over, facing them so they are upright towards her. The first card is **"Change"** with a chameleon on it. The second card is

"**Desire**" with a leopard on it. The third and final card is "**Happiness**" with a bumblebee on it.

"The first card we have here is change, something is stirring up to change in your life. The second card being desire, it is going to be something you've either been working towards or something you've wanted for a while." A few people around us are looking at the cards in awe, while others still look unsure. Clara's eyes are focused on the cards, like she's trying to pull her own meanings from them. "It will lead to feeling more happy, and since it is something you've wanted for a while, it's going to affect your whole life in a great way." A lot of wows, and chatter starts after I finish her reading.

"Millie proposed earlier today at brunch." She says, holding out her left hand for me to see the ring. Everyone around us gasps with surprise and shock.

"And you're just now telling me?!" I playfully yell at her.

"We didn't want to ruin your birthday tomorrow." She says nervously.

"Are you kidding? If anything, this is the best birthday gift ever!" I yell, jumping up and hugging her. I wave Millie over to join the hug. "My best friends are getting married!" I'm so happy for them!

We spend the rest of the night celebrating their engagement with drinks and games.

Chapter Two
Sage's 25th Birthday
Halloween

My phone vibrating on its wireless charger is what wakes me. I rub my tired eyes, and look at the time, *9:34*. I sigh, I should be awake by now anyway. The caller ID reads "Mom" I grab my phone off the stand and answer it.

"Hello?" I say, yawning.

"I'm sorry sweetie, did I wake you?"

"Yeah, but it's fine. I should've been awake already."

"Well I just wanted to call and wish you a happy birthday. Will you stop by later? Grams and I want to talk to you about something." She says sounding nervous.

"Thanks mom. How about I come for dinner around five?" I ask.

"That would be perfect. We will see you then. Love you, honey."

"Love you too, mom." We hang up, so I decide it's time to get up and start my day. I climb out of bed, grabbing my favorite dress from my closet. It's half black and half red with a zipper down the middle separating the colors. I grab some undergarments and head for the bathroom. I take a quick fifteen minute shower, and get dressed after drying off. I smell eggs and bacon from my

bathroom, after I'm ready for the day I head out to
the kitchen.

"Good morning birthday girl!" Clara yells, as
she's cooking eggs. Millie is setting the table with
plates, cups and silverware.

"Happy birthday Sagie!" Millie says, looking
up from the table. "We made you breakfast!"

"Aw, you guys are my favorite, you didn't
have to do that." I say, forcing them both into a hug.
They laugh and say a chorus of things like 'we
wanted to', and 'you deserve it.' We sit down at the
table and talk about what the day holds. Millie has
to work at the cafe from eleven until four. Clara and
I are going to go shopping for a costume to wear to
my birthday and halloween party tonight around
ten. I tell them I have to meet my mom and grams
for dinner, so they don't make any plans including
me.

I've lived with Clara and Millie since our
sophomore year of college. They own this house,
and I'm just here until they kick me out, decide to
have kids, or I chose to move out on my own. I
don't see them ever kicking me out, though.

Millie leaves for work after we clean up the
kitchen. Clara goes to their room to get ready to go
shopping. When she's ready, we head to our local
outdoor outlet mall. There's a few places at that
mall that we can get costumes at. She parks her car,
and we start making our way to the first store. A
man's shoulder hits me, an accident I'm sure, but
when his shoulder hits mine, I gasp. *I see a
meatball sub in his hand, he takes a bite of it and*

collapses to the ground. He spits out the bite he took, he holds his chest gasping for air. I see him pass away.

"Sage? What's wrong?" Clara asks, making the daydream, nightmare, or whatever that was go away.

"Sorry," the man mutters as he walks by me.

"I just saw that man die of a heart attack, but it hasn't happened yet." I say to Clara. We turn to face him, he's still walking away from us. He is holding a meatball sub. He takes a bite before turning back towards us. His face is pale, and his facial expression is scared, shocked, or he's choking. Was I wrong? Is he not having a heart attack? His right hand grabs his chest where his heart is. Oh shit. He collapses onto the pavement, gasping for air.

"Call 911!" I yell to Clara, she nods quickly in a panic. I'm a little rusty, but I manage to get him breathing again right when a paramedic shows up. I see a shadowy figure behind the paramedic. He's dressed in a black robe, and is holding a scythe. I have got to be dreaming right now. I can't see his face. It's Halloween, it's just a teenager or some adult worker dressed up. It's gotta be. I walk over to him, leaving Clara behind.

"What the fuck is wrong with you?!" I whisper-yell at him. I don't want to cause more of a scene. "Why didn't you come try to help, or just go about your business? Are you some sort of sicko who gets off on people almost dying?! That's a little morbid that you are dressed as a reaper as someone just about died."

"You can see me?" He asks, his face now looking at me, and revealing itself. His skin tone is pale, but not in a sick kind of way. He has these electrifying bright blue eyes, and a nice sharp jawline. His hair blonde is parted to one side, but mostly covered by his hood. He's attractive. I want to admire him forever, but I'm livid.

"Are you insane? Of course I can see you!" I whisper yell still. He grabs my arm and pulls me down a hallway that leads to one of the bathrooms.

"No, I'm not insane. You just saved the man I was supposed to reap, darling. His time was up." I laugh coldly. This has to be some sick joke.

"You're horrible! That's not funny."

"I'm not trying to be funny. I'm seriously a reaper."

"Yeah, okay, and I'm the Queen of England." I shake my head, and go to walk away. He grabs my arm.

"Let me show you," He doesn't let go of my arm. We are no longer in the hallway of the outdoor mall. We're standing on a beach now, it looks like the East Coast.

"The next person on my list is going to drown. No one can see us right now. No one can ever see me, so I'm not sure how you are able to."

"How? What?" My mind is racing. I have no words to say besides those two, I have no idea what to ask or what to do.

He shows me what happens when he reaps. There's a woman with her brown hair pulled back in the ocean. The waves pull her under, she's trying to wave her hands for help but no one sees her. I try to run towards her, but I can't move. When her body is pulled out of the water, a lifeguard on the beach tries to preform CPR. It doesn't work. Lux uses the scythe to lift her soul from her body, he doesn't touch her body at all, the scythe sucks the soul from the body as Lux holds it over her chest. The slightly glowing soul goes into the scythe.

"I move on to the next person after I'm done." He shrugs.

"How do you know who is next and where to go? Do you do this 24/7?" I ask, only a couple of my million questions pouring out. He pulls out a phone. A freaking phone. I think I'm going to pass out. I steady myself. "You have a phone?!"

"I'm half human, half reaper. I can make myself known to people, like let them see me when I want them to."

"So you're like a ghost from that one show, *American Horror Story*?" He laughs.

"Yeah kind of, but I'm not a ghost. I have to fulfill my reaper duties during the day, and I can be a 'normal' human at the end of the day." I'm baffled. I think my jaw is ajar, not at the ground yet but close. "I'm immortal though, so I'm not allowed to fall in love with a human, it's against the rules."

"Whose rules?"

"Um, I'm not really allowed to answer that."

"Ugh!" I'm so frustrated, so confused.

"So, what are you?" He asks, his eyebrows raised. Now what the fuck is this man, reaper, person talking about?

"Um, a human named Sage."

"Sage, that's pretty. What's your last name?"

"Um, is that any of your business? How do I know you aren't going to add me to your list?"

"Just tell me, please. I have a job I need to get back to soon. I can't just add people to the list. You also say 'um' too much." He rolls his eyes and scoffs..

"Nolan."

"Nolan? Like Rena Nolan?" he asks, looking up from his phone and at me again.

"How do you know my grandma's name?"

"Well that answers my question about what you are."

"What the fuck, man! I'm very clearly a human." He laughs. He's fucking laughing at me.

"Yeah okay. Whatever helps you sleep at night." He grabs my arm again, and we appear back at the mall. Just like a snap of the fingers. Poof.

"So, what am I?" I ask him, after he lets go of my arm.

"Not my place to tell, darling, but what I do know is I will be seeing you again. The name's Lux by the way." With that, he disappears. I'm frustrated, confused, and lost. I know where I am, but I feel lost, like there's a family secret. Is that why my mom sounded so nervous this morning? Whatever, I'll try to act normal with Clara, and get a costume. After we decide what costumes we want to get, I will head straight to my moms after we get back home. Even if it's earlier than five like we discussed.

I walk back over to Clara who is still talking to an officer. They both look at me, confused.

"Where did you go?" Clara asks me, and the officer clearly also wants to know.

"To the bathroom, sorry. I haven't done CPR since the training I did a few years ago. It made me nauseous that I actually had to do it on someone."

"Are you feeling better now?" She asks.

"A little." I don't want to tell her what really happened, not yet anyway. The officer wants to ask me a few questions, I nod. I think I dissociated during most of the questions so I don't know what I answered. Finally, Clara and I are free to continue our shopping adventure. She doesn't push me to talk about how I knew what would happen, or how I'm feeling which I'm thankful for. I wouldn't even know where to start if she did try to push me to talk. I'll tell her at some point, but right now I think it's best I process this first.

We finally reach one of the Halloween stores, my mind is so frazzled that I don't even know where I want to start. Clara heads for the more slutty, but cute costumes.

"I think if I got something like this Millie would just rip it right off me." She holds up a costume that reads "Sexy Nurse," and it shows a lot of cleavage. I roll my eyes, what a typical slutty costume. I don't know why people insist on turning important jobs like that into something inappropriate. "Ooo what about this one?" She holds up a "Sexy Female Devil." I roll my eyes yet again.

"You'd pull it off, but you're also going to have Millie glaring at every single person that looks your way." She laughs.

"You are totally right, but I love when she is protective like that towards me. It's a turn on." She giggles.

"I didn't need to know that." I say, shaking my head. I start walking to the fairy costumes.

"There's no such thing as TMI in our friendship." She says, trailing behind me, still holding the devil costume.

"Is that what you're getting?" I point to it.

"Yup." She pops her P. "Now we have to find something for you to wear." She goes on a hunt for stuff she thinks I will wear, as I keep browsing the fairy outfits. They're all cute, but they aren't screaming at me. I really shouldn't care what I look like, I have no one to impress or to even try to impress.

I don't have anyone in my life that is interested in me, and I'm not interested in anyone. I walk to the next aisle, I'm no longer in the fairies. The first costume that catches my eye is a freaking grim reaper costume, and I'm not talking like the robes, and scythe like Lux was wearing, I'm talking like a corset, and it shows more than I normally would. It's called the "Glammed Reaper", it's a corset dress with fishnet leggings connected. I do have to say, it is pretty and kind of ironic after the morning I've had.

Clara skips over with a couple costumes in her hand, not including hers. She holds them out for me to see. The first one she brought over as a joke, it's a banana. The second one is actually cute, it's an Egyptian Princess.

"I grabbed the banana cause you never show your rocking body off." She says, I scoff.

"I do too. Just occasionally, and my body is not rocking." I say to her, before turning around and grabbing the reaper costume to show her. "Do you think this is too much? Is wrong after what happened this morning?"

"Girl not at all! I think it's perfect, you should get it. Oh! You'll want this too." She says, before grabbing a scythe from the shelf of accessories. I want to hit my forehead with my hand, but I don't. I can't get this, I literally bitched at Lux earlier for dressing the way he was when that man almost died. I feel like I would be a hypocrite if I got this costume. Fuck it. It's hot, and like Clara said, I need to show off my quote on quote, rocking body. I grab the scythe from her.

She puts the banana and Egyptian Princess back where she got them and we head to the checkout. She insists on buying my costume as 'part of my birthday gift'. We leave the store, and decide not to check out any other places since I want to go to my mom's as soon as possible now. We get back to our house, and I head to my room throwing the costume on my bed. I look at myself in my mirror, I look tired, and I feel tired. It just came out of nowhere. I look at the time, *12:32*. It's still early, so I'm going to take a quick nap before I head to my moms.

Chapter Three

My alarm goes off at two, I want to snooze it, but I also want to get to my mom's. I debate my options, getting up or sleeping a little longer. Ugh, I suppose I will get up. I throw the same outfit I was wearing before I stripped for my nap. I grab my keys, plus my purse and head out the door. My mom doesn't live far, maybe ten minutes away. I will admit that I don't visit as much as I should anymore, but she understands.

My nerves are on the rise the closer I get to her house. I don't know why I am this nervous. I pull onto her street, her and my grandma's cars sit in her driveway. I pull in behind my moms car, putting my own car into park. I turn off the engine, and take a deep breath. It's going to be fine, everything is going to be fine. I step in the front door, I'm hit with the smell of some kind of incense. My mom is always burning some kind of incense, or a candle, sometimes even both. My mom and Grams are both sitting in the kitchen playing cards.

"Whose winning?" I ask, sitting down beside Grams. Both of them jump a little, whoops, I didn't mean to scare them.

"I am, and you're early." Grams says, pulling me into her side for a small hug.

"Yeah, sorry. I had a crazy thing happen at the mall today. I decided to take a nap as soon as I got back to my place, before coming here. I figured

I'd better get here as soon as possible after what happened. I thought it might have something to do with what mom wanted to tell me." I say.

"What happened?" My mom asks, standing up and walking over to give me a hug from the side as well. They both didn't give me the chance to stand to give them proper hugs. I tell them everything, every detail I can recall. I stare at the table as I tell the story of the events of this morning. His face coming back to my mind, the reaper. There was something about him, and he knows my grandma.

"Ah, so you met Lux?" Grams asks, breaking me from my thoughts after I spilled the story.

"What are we? How do you know each other? Why am I just now finding all of this out?" I ask, as more questions arise in my head.

"Sweetheart, we are psychics." My mom answers, laughing.

"Psychics? Like those people that read people's energy and fortune?"

"In a way. You already do that with your cards, but now your gifts are completely opened as of today. Your twenty-fifth birthday. It's when everyone in our family receives their gifts." My mom says.

"Each psychic in the family has their own unique gift, though. Your mom can see events that happened in the past. I can see the dead. You apparently can see how people are going to die when you touch them."

"But how come it didn't happen when I hugged you two?" I ask.

"It happens when it needs to, or maybe since your gift is still growing it'll take time to work on every person you touch." Grams says. "We haven't had anyone in the family, that I'm aware of, have that gift before, but it could be in the family book. I never had the time to finish it. It has all of our family history in it." I nod. This is all very interesting and kind of scary. It makes sense though, seeing the guy die before it actually happened, seeing death.

"How do you know Lux?"

"Sweetie girl, I can see the dead, so obviously I can see reapers too."

"But he is half human."

"Yes, but even during his reaper form as we will call it, I can still see him. That's just how our gifts work."

"Grams, how do you know him?" My grams sighs before looking towards my mom, who then nods at her. Oh my gosh, what are they hiding from me now?!

"You don't remember it, we found someone in our family, a distant cousin who has the ability to erase memories from one's mind. Ten years ago today, on your fifteenth birthday we had a pool party to celebrate." Grams starts. "Your friends from school all came, you were having the best time, but you were clumsy. You tripped over a rock, right as you caught your balance you lost it again by falling into the pool only to hit your head really hard on the diving board. That end of the pool was seven feet deep, we made sure you kids didn't go on that end of the pool unless you knew how to swim, which you did but the hit knocked you unconscious." I'm slowly taking it all in. Grams grabs my hand to show support.

"No one saw it happen in real time, we only know what really happened because of your mom's gift. You drowned, Sage. You died for two minutes and fifty-seven seconds. I saw Lux, he wasn't much older than you then, not by the looks of him anyway. Your mom did CPR as your five friends at your party stood around shocked and not sure what to do." Grams pauses again, her eyes are watering now. Mom is covering her mouth with her hand, her eyes also watering. "I went over to Lux, I begged him to save you. I knew you were destined to be here longer, and he did too. Your mom, and he saved you that day. We had to make you, and all your friends forget what happened that day. We didn't know what they saw, and we didn't want you to be scared of the pool. We shouldn't have used powers like that. We did what we thought was right. I'm so sorry we never told you about any of this until now."

I'm frozen in the chair. I don't know what to say right away. Grams and mom are both crying. I'm just trying to soak it all in. I take a deep breath, and try to keep myself from crying.

"So that's how he knew what I am, what we are, because he's met us before." Grams nods.

"Not just once either, he's been here a few times. Like when your grandpa died, and years later your dad. Lux came both times." My grandpa died almost eight years ago, and it's been almost two years since my dad passed. I frown at the remembrance of their passing, sometimes it feels like they're just away at work, or the store. "Don't be sad honey, they're always with and around you."

"At least you can still see and talk to them." I say to Grams. It comes out harsher than I meant it to.

"Not all the time, sweetie. It doesn't always work that way." She says, as my mom serves up dinner for us to eat. We chat about what they know about our family, some of the other gifts, and how I need to allow mine to grow. 'Don't fight your gifts, they are meant to shine bright.' Grams reminds me before I walk out the door to get ready for my birthday celebration tonight. It's seven when I leave their house, and knowing Clara, she'll have the party starting around nine.

☠ ☠

When I get inside the house, Clara and Millie are setting up Halloween and birthday decorations. I can't help but laugh, they don't go together at all, which I should be used to by now.

"Hey! No peeking!' Clara shouts at me as she tries to hide some of the decorations with her hands. I laugh.

"It's a little late for that." I say, as I walk into my room. "Don't worry, I'm going to go get ready. You keep decorating."

"Don't come out until we give you the okay!" Clara shouts at me from the living room.

"Yeah, yeah, whatever." I yell back, laughing. I put my costume on first, trying not to let my thoughts get to me.

I'm still experiencing some regret about getting this costume, but it's so cute. The costume hugs my body, and definitely shows a lot of cleavage. You only live once, though so fuck it. I decide to do my makeup next, I start with black eyeshadow doing half of each eyelid closer to my nose, and then I do a sliver glittery eyeshadow on the other side of my eyelid. I mix the two in the middle, making it look smokey and perfect. I add some eyeliner with mascara. My blue eyes are popping now. I finish off with some black lipstick, a girl can never wear too much black.

When I'm officially satisfied with my look, I snap a few quick selfies that help build my confidence more. I look hot. Not long later, Clara comes barging in my room, looking like a badass. I knew she'd look good in the sexy devil costume.

"What does Millie think of that outfit?" I ask her, not even bothering to ask her why she barged in.

"Well she stood behind me while I did my makeup and drooled for like five minutes." She says laughing. "She's definitely ripping this off me tonight like I knew she would."

"LALALA." I yell holding my ears tight with my hands.

"No TMI between us, remember?" She yells right next to my ear.

"Yeah, yeah, whatever." I say with a dismissive wave. "Who is all coming tonight?"

"Millie's cousin, some of his friends, some of our friends, and whoever they end up telling." She shrugs. Great, people we don't know. It'll be fine, my anxiety will go away after a drink or two.

"Okay."

"Your costume is hella cute on you." Clara says, looking at it more. "Plus your makeup is perfect."

"Thanks, I still have this guilt of getting it."

"Why?" I don't want to explain to her what happened, but she's my best friend so she will understand.

"You should sit." I motion for the chair behind her. She nods and sits down in it. I sit on the edge of my bed facing her. I tell her everything that happened earlier, and how the visit went with my grandmother and mom. She listens to it, and doesn't interrupt.

"Wow." She says when I get done explaining what unfolded today. "That's all I can think of to say to that. I'm literally speechless."

"It's a lot, trust me I know." I laugh.

"You're holding and taking it well. I think I'd freak the fuck out." She laughs.

"I'm kinda shocked that I'm not."

"Your family hasn't told you anything before this?"

"Nope. They don't tell anyone in the family until their twenty-fifth birthday when their 'powers' come to light."

"Wow." She says again. I nod.

"Yeah. Pretty crazy."

"You aren't crazy. I think you have an amazing gift, herb." I roll my eyes at the nickname she knows I hate.

"Amazing? It's scary as fuck."

"It's amazing, because do you realize how many people you could save before they die?!" She stands up. "You can help so many people."

"Yeah, you're right." My mind goes to Lux, wouldn't that mess with his job though?. Oh well, I can save people.

"Come on, I need to show you something!" Clara says, taking my mind away from Lux again. She grabs my arm, and leads me out to the living room. It looks amazing, decorations are everywhere. A mix between birthday and Halloween, a good mix. I smile.

"Thank you, this looks perfect!" Clara cheers, jumping up and down.

"Did you hear her, Mills?! She thinks it looks perfect." I laugh, and so does Millie.

"Yes, my love. I heard her." Millie comes over and pulls her in for a side hug, planting a kiss on her head. "You did a great job."

"We did." She adds, making Millie smile more.

The house fills up fast with guests, and people wanting to have a good time. Some tell me happy birthday while others just ask where the booze is. I direct them to the kitchen, and laugh to myself. I make my way through the crowd after grabbing my own drink, a *Malibu Sunset* that Clara made me. She definitely added more alcohol than I would have, but it's my birthday so fuck it. I throw myself on the living room couch. People dance to the music around me.

I take a big sip of my drink, then close my eyes and enjoy the beat of the music. I feel the music in my body, music is my therapy, it soothes my soul and eases my mind. The couch sinks beside me, but I don't open my eyes.

"Nice costume." A male voice yells from beside me, making sure I can hear him. "I'm pretty sure you gave me shit about my outfit earlier, and here you are wearing a sexy cheap halloween costume version." I hear part anger, part amusement in his voice. I open one eye to see who is sitting beside me, and open them both when I realize it's Lux. He is dressed up as the *"Phantom"* from *The Phantom of the Opera*, one of my favorite musicals. I want to swoon, but I am so irritated with him and his existence I ignore his costume for now. I scoff, and roll my eyes.

"I thought it was cute, and for your information, I felt guilty getting it. I also felt guilty putting it on, but I don't know why I am even bothering to explain myself to you. It's not like I can exchange it now." The sensitive girl inside of me wants to cry, but the anger part of me wants to yell more at him.

"Woah, it's not that big of a deal. All I was doing was messing with you, and trying to get you to feel what I felt, in a way."

"Well I hope you're happy, because it worked. Now I don't want to be at my own birthday party so thank you so fucking much." I get up, and start heading to my room.

"Wait." He calls out, trying to catch up to me. I slam my door closed before he can catch up to me. My door slamming didn't affect the party going on the other side as the music is still blaring and voices still chatting. I faceplant into my bed, and cry. The tears I cry are not only sad, they're also anger and frustration. I knew this costume would be a mistake. Who knew how much a mess my life would be at the fresh age of twenty-five? How is it possible that in less than a day, I no longer feel I have control in my life? I'm twenty-five now, I shouldn't be this much of a crybaby, but I'm going to allow myself to feel my emotions. The bed sinks beside me.

"I didn't mean to upset you. You look stunning." A deep, but soothing voice says beside me. Lux. "I just had to give you shit like you did to me earlier. I didn't realize it was your birthday. I apologize for hurting you."

"I don't want your fucking apology. Just go enjoy the party, and leave me alone." I'm no longer upset, just angry. Who does he think he is just walking into my room? Once he leaves without another word, I wait a bit before sneaking out of my room to down some more drinks. I need to get drunk, I need to escape my feelings and thoughts.

I down three of my favorite drinks, and before I know it all my angry thoughts are gone. I wonder where Clara and Millie are. I make my way out of the kitchen and into the living room. The music and people dancing shake the floor, and I stumble some but don't totally lose my balance. I don't see Clara and Millie in the living room.

I don't bother looking in their room or outside, so I plop back onto the couch. My mind goes back to Lux, seeing him in the *'Phantom'* outfit, he looked sexy. I hit my head with my palm, trying to knock the thought I just had out of my head. He is fine, and I am so drawn to him, but he has royally pissed me off many times in less than twenty-four hours. I can't be around someone that gets on my nerves that much.

He is a reaper for crying out loud, I don't think he is allowed to be with anyone. Wait, now why am I thinking we could be something one day?! I look in my cup, my fourth drink is almost gone. I finish the last few sips, and throw the cup away.

I don't need anymore drinks right now, or maybe even for the night. I see Clara and Millie walking out of their room, hand in hand, smiling and talking. They see me, before making their way to the couch and sitting down beside me.

"Who was that guy in the *'Phantom'* costume?" Clara asks, wiggling her eyebrows. "We know you love the *'Phantom,'* and that guy totally had the hots for you. We watched him admire you from across the room until he finally made his way to the couch beside you. We walked away after that to do our own activities."

"Gross, I don't need to know that you guys just had sex."

"Oh we didn't." Clara says with a wink, before looking at her fiance. "Anyways, back to the hottie that was admiring you." I roll my eyes.

"He's not hot, and he definitely wasn't admiring me. It was Lux." I explain to her. She gasps.

"The reaper?!" She says a little too loud, which causes people to look in her direction.

"Shush!" I say back. She whispers a quick sorry. "Yes, the reaper. The one that I bitched out earlier." Millie doesn't look confused, so I know Clara told her which is fine.

"Dude, he totally wants you." Clara says, I roll my eyes again.

"No he is just trying to get back at me for saving that man earlier." I say, closing my eyes. "Plus I threw this huge fit earlier, like a big crybaby. No guy likes shit like that." She laughs.

"You are allowed to have and express emotions. Everyone expresses them differently."

"Yeah, I guess so." I shrug. She bumps her shoulder into mine.

"Cheer up, it's your birthday and that man definitely has the hots for you. If you don't want to see that yet, that's on you." She sticks her tongue out at me. "Seriously though, have some fun before I force you."

"Fine, fine." I get up and start dancing. Clara joins me, making me dance with her. The music is loud, fast paced, and is a vibe.

After an hour of dancing, Clara and Millie get everyone's attention for them to cut a cake, and make me open gifts. Gifts they shouldn't have gotten me. They bought a huge sheet cake, and plan to cut it into small pieces so there is enough for everyone here. Clara lights the candles on the cake, before directing everyone to start singing 'Happy Birthday' to me.

Everyone's eyes are on me, I hate it, but this is so damn sweet of my friends. The cake has light blue frosting, with *Happy 25th Birthday Sage* in purple frosting. There are little balloons in the corner, one a darker blue, a light purple, and a sage green. I can't help but laugh a little that they managed to get that shade of green on my cake.

I blow out all the candles when they finish singing. Cake gets passed around once it's cut, I get the biggest piece since it is my birthday cake, after all. When everyone goes back to partying, Clara and Millie come back onto the couch beside me. Clara sits on Millie's lap, Clara is facing me. They are each holding medium boxes, wrapped in lilac wrapping paper. Clara hands me the box she's holding first.

"Open mine first!" She pushes it into my hands. I laugh, shaking my head but take it from her.

"You guys didn't have to get me anything." I say, looking up from the box.

"We wanted to!" Millie says, and nods at me to open it. I rip the wrapping paper off the box before opening the box to find a super cute black cardigan. I love cardigans, and almost always have one on.

"This is perfect! It'll go with every outfit. Thank you Clara!" I say, hugging her while she still sits on Millie's lap.

"Here open mine now," Millie hands me the box that was sitting beside her and Clara. Ripping the wrapping paper off the second gift, and opening the box, I find a book. It's the next romance novel I've been wanting to get. It even has decorative edges, it is beautiful.

"Open the cover." Millie says. I do as she says and open the cover. O.M.G. It's signed by the author, my favorite author ever, *Jeanne Rivered.*

"How did you get this signed?!" I'm freaking out internally.

"A friend of Clara's went to a book signing of hers, and we knew she was your favorite author so I paid the friend to get an extra copy for you. It's really not that big of a deal." Millie shrugs.

"Not that big of a deal. These are two of the best gifts ever. I'm so blessed to have friends like you two. Thank you!" I pull them both in an awkward hug that leaves Clara in the middle. "Thank you for this amazing party. I think I'm going to head to bed. I love you both."

"Wait before you go to bed, we have one more gift for you, but it won't happen for a couple months, the concert is in December." Clara says, standing up with me. She pulls an envelope out of her costume, a smart place to hide it. I open the envelope. Oh my goodness, tickets to a concert, and not just any concert. I get to see my favorite band live, *5 Seconds Of Summer*.

"No fucking way. Seriously you two are the best friends on the planet." I pull them into another hug. "Thank you, thank you! You both are coming with me right?!"

"Just me, Millie isn't really into their music like we are." Clara says, shrugging.

"I'm so excited! Thank you both for the best birthday." I give them each one last hug individually before heading to my room. Today was a crazy eventful, but overall good day. I can't help but smile like an idiot until I fall asleep.

Chapter Four

I've never been much of a runner, but for some reason I'm running on the trail in the nearby park. The early morning seven am breeze feels nice on my face, and on the sweat dripping down my face. The trees are changing colors, orange and reds fill the limbs, and are starting to litter the ground. The fall weather is gorgeous, I am so not ready for winter. I see someone running in front of me, her blue hair is recognizable from anywhere. She works at the coffee shop Clara and I go pretty often. Her name is Sandra. She's sweet, but I don't know her too well. She's at least a half mile in front of me. Out of nowhere, she trips over something on the ground and her head hits the concrete trail hard. Very hard. Her body goes limp, I pick up my pace, and get to her as quickly as I can. I check her pulse, she's gone. Fuck. I grab my phone and dial 911. I tell the operator what happened. They're sending help that should be here in less than five minutes. Before I can start CPR, I feel a presence behind me.

"I wouldn't do what you're thinking about doing." Lux says, knowing I'm about to perform CPR on her.

That's when I wake up. I sit up fast, what the fuck was that?! Was that a premonition? I can fucking dream them and see them without touching someone? I look at the time on my phone, *6:30.*

Only one way to find out, this time if it is real, I am going to save her.

I throw on some comfy exercise clothes, leggings and a sports bra. I don't run a lot, so I don't have a fancy matching outfit. My sports bra is purple, obviously my favorite color, and black leggings. I head to the park, and start running. I get to the spot where Sandra hits her head. There's a bench a few feet away, I sit on it and check my phone while I wait.

Just like my dream, I see her running, but this time towards me instead of in front of me. She's a pretty fast runner, and that's when I notice it. The concrete is uneven in the spot she hits, she must have stepped down and went to lift her foot up and caught it just right. How in the world am I going to prevent her from falling? Catch her? Maybe I can 'accidentally' bump into her causing her to get distracted by the uneven cement. It's worth a shot, before she gets close to it, I get up and start running towards her. I pretend to look at my phone, and run into her shoulder. She scoffs, and lands on her butt. That is a lot better than her head like my dream.

"Oh my gosh, I'm so sorry. I looked down quickly to look at my heart rate and didn't see you. Are you okay?" I ask her, extending my hand to help her up. She accepts my hand, and she gets up.

"My butt might bruise, but otherwise I'm okay. Try to be a little more careful when you check your heart rate next time." She says with a smile, finally looking at me. I laugh at her bruised butt comment. "Wait, you come in with your friend to the coffee shop I work at all the time. I've never seen you run out here before."

"I drank a lot last night at my birthday party, so I decided to try a run to help my hangover." I'm not completely lying, I did drink last night, but I definitely didn't drink enough to be hungover. She laughs. Okay good, she bought that.

"Be careful, there's an uneven chunk of concrete up there. I almost tripped on it. You don't need to bruise your ass more." I joke.

"Thanks! I'll make sure to look out for it. I hope your run helps your hangover!" She says before returning to her run. She successfully makes it over the uneven spot. She's safe.

"You gotta be fucking joking." Lux says from behind me. I turn to face him.

"What?" I ask innocently.

"You are taking my job away from me."

"I'm saving people. People that have families, people that deserve to live longer, good people." He rolls his eyes.

"You can't keep messing with fate like this. You're going to fuck shit up, Sage."

"This isn't *Final Destination*, Lux. This is real life." This earns me another eye roll, he gets close to me, and I mean face to face.

"You can't keep saving the people I need to reap. They are meant to pass and move on. If you keep doing this, it isn't going to end well, so do us both a favor and stop, now!" His face is serious, his bright blue eyes are stone cold, and he is pissed. "I can reap anyone at any time, dead or alive. Don't make me reap you, because I am not afraid to one, get my hands dirty, and two reap an alive psychic human. I've reaped a living before, and I will do it again if I have to." He's trying to scare me. I roll my eyes.

"Whatever, I will do what I want and you can't stop me."

"I literally just told you I can and will stop you." I back up.

"I'd love to see you try." I take off running, the opposite direction from him. He appears in front of me, and I run into him. I fall to the ground on my butt, just like Sandra did.

"You're such an asshole."

"I can be a bigger one. Do as I say, Sage or things aren't going to end pretty." With that, he disappears. I stand up, before brushing my legs and ass off from the rocks I fell on. I want to punch him so bad. I finish my run on the trail before heading to the coffee shop. I want to surprise Clara and Millie with their usual coffee. Sandra is working at the register. Is she going to think I followed her? No, no, Clara and I come here a lot. It's fine, it's all going to be fine.

I order our three drinks, and head home. Sandra acted normal, and I tried my best to be as normal as possible. I'm just awkward, and I just saved her life in a way, whether she realizes it or not. I walked to the park this morning, to the trail, so now I'm walking back home with a carrier with the three coffees in it.

While walking, my mind can't help but think of Lux. When did he become a reaper? How did he become one? If he is half-human, half-reaper why did he decide to be a reaper now instead of waiting until he was at the end of his human days to become a reaper? This is still all so weird and confusing to me. I just want to go back to living my normal life. Tomorrow is Monday, I'll just pretend my life is still normal. I'll go back to work, and focus on helping students, their parents, and other school office stuff. I'm a secretary at the local high school. I'm hoping to get the school counselor position next year.

I have my masters so I can be one, but our school's current one is sticking around until she is forced to retire or dies. That's actually kind of dark to think about. I don't know why my mind went there, but it's wrong.

I get the coffees safely in the house without dropping any, and give them to the girls. They are grateful for the coffees, but have to get on the road to go to Millie's family's house. Her aunt just passed away, so they're going a few hours away to the funeral. They are staying the whole week, so I will have the house to myself. That doesn't make me nervous at all. My phone buzzes in my pocket.

Clara: Don't hesitate to text me if you need anything.
Me: Thanks love

They just left not even five minutes ago, and seeing how she sent me that right after leaving proves how well she knows me. I smile a little, and then hop on our couch. They cleaned up the party late last night after everyone left. I'm not sure how they have the energy to drive three hours this morning, even with the coffee. Time to spend the day rotting on the couch.

The day passed by fast, even with me just chilling on the couch. It's almost dinner time now, and I have no idea what I'm going to eat. The doorbell rings, knocking me out of my thoughts of food. Who in the world is here right now? I look through the peep hole in the door. Lux. I roll my eyes. Great, so much for spending most of my day relaxing after this morning incident. I open the door a little bit.

"What do you want?" I don't hide my annoyed tone. He's dressed in black skinny jeans, and a black short sleeve. His blonde hair is combed to the side, and his light tan skin is glowing in the dawn light.

"I came by to talk." He says simply. You gotta do better than that, buddy.

"About?" I'm only getting more annoyed.

"This morning, the mall, everything." His eyes haven't met mine yet, they stay looking above my head or at the door.

"Can it wait? I'd rather just ignore this new aspect of my life, and go back to living how I did normally."

"Sage, that isn't possible anymore. Your life is never going to be the way it used to. I know that probably hurts to hear, but it's the truth. Sometimes the truth hurts." He says, shrugging. He can be such a dick. I go to close the door, but he puts his hand out, stopping it from closing between us. "Please let me explain."

I really just wanted to spend the rest of my night watching TV, and eating junk food before it's back to work for the week.

"Please, Sage." He says, finally looking at me. Those blue eyes are seriously intoxicating, and compelling.

"Ugh, fine, but you get no more than thirty minutes. After thirty minutes, you're leaving."

"I can probably work with that."

"Probably?" I raise my eyebrow.

"I can work with that." I open the door to let him in. He walks in, and heads for the couch. He sits down exactly where I was sitting.

"You're in my spot."

"What are you Sheldon from *The Big Bang Theory*?"

"No, that's just where I was sitting before you rudely interrupted my lazy night." He moves over, so I can have my spot back. "Do you want a drink?"

"No thank you. I'd rather just be able to get everything out that I need to before my thirty minutes are up." I nod, sitting down unfortunately beside him in my original spot.

"Alright, your thirty minutes starts now." I look at the time, five forty-five.

"I'm not sure where to start, so I'm going to start from the beginning. Did your mom and grandmother tell you that we have met before?"

"Yeah, they told me yesterday when I saw them."

"Okay good. I didn't want to be the one to tell that story, as it isn't my place to tell." I nod. He goes on, "So the beginning, twenty-five years ago I was born, on the same day as you, Sage. My mom died during childbirth. No one knew my dad. A lot of people in the hospital joked that my dad was Death himself. My uncle took me in, and raised me until he died when I was ten. That's when I started hearing this voice, I know it sounds crazy so bear with me, this voice told me I was chosen to help people move on when they die." Lux pauses, looking at me. I'm looking at him intrigued. The way his mouth moves when he talks is so attractive. His blue eyes sparkly in the lighting.

"Every morning, I hear the list of names of people that are going to die. I type them out in my notes app on my phone, and cross them off after the reaping. I've never seen this voice. Since this started, I really began to believe that my uncle and everyone at the hospital was right, that I'm the son of Death. The voice told me I'd be immortal and wouldn't age past thirty, as long as I chose to continue to be a reaper." He sighs, he's looking down at his hands.

"I'm also not allowed to fall in love. I can have a semi-normal human life, without being with another human. I met you at your birthday party when you drowned. They begged for your life back. I was drawn to you, there was just something about you that made me curious. I knew your family had a history of powerful psychics, but didn't know that it was passed down to every daughter in the family. I granted them your life back. I'm only allowed to do that five times in my entire time of being a reaper. Five. You're the only one I've chosen to bring back, in the last fifteen years of me doing this." He looks down at his hands the rest of the time as he tells me about his crazy life.

"Wow. Where did you stay after your uncle passed away?"

"I bounced around to a lot of foster homes. I would skip school to do my reaping duties. I would come home late. It got me and some of my foster families into trouble, but I couldn't explain this to them." I nod. It must have been tough to go through what he did at such a young age.

"I'm sorry you went through that."

"Thanks, it wasn't easy at first."

"I bet. Why are you telling me all of this?"

"I told you, I've been drawn to you since the day we met."

"I don't remember you then, sure they told me about it happening, but I don't remember the details myself."

"I just feel like I have to get to know you more." That's when the light bulb in my head flips on. I can't believe I didn't notice it before. How did I not?

"Oh no, I know what this is. You're just trying to get close to me so I don't save the people you're supposed to reap. Do you think I'm dumb?" I'm starting to get angry.

"No, I don't think you're dumb. I seriously just want to get to know you." I shake my head. I take a deep breath to prevent myself from getting any angrier.

"Get out."

"What?" His shocked facial expression only pisses me off more. "It hasn't been thirty minutes yet."

"It's been close enough. Now get out before I call the cops." He scrambles up, before leaving. I lock the door behind him. I will not let someone try to get in my head like that. After I kick him out, I feel a little guilty about how I reacted. My emotions just fluctuate so bad. One minute I can be happy, and the next minute I'm fuming with anger.

Now, it's time to spend the rest of the night eating tacos I'm going to now have delivered and watch more tv. I can't believe he had the nerve to just show up like that, but at the same time I'm glad he told me all of that, even if it was some twisted way to get closer to me.

After I kicked Lux out last night, I ordered way too much food and watched movies until I needed to go to bed. This morning I woke up dreading to get out of my bed. My life is supposed to go back to normal today, that's what I told myself. I know that it's never going to be the same again though. It's almost like grief.

Oddly enough, I'm stuck with this gift forever, like I will always have the grief of my dad and grandpa. It will never go away, even when people say it will eventually. That's the biggest lie I've ever fucking heard. You just learn how to live with it, but it'll always be with you. They will never come back no matter how much I cry, but the crying helps me feel like they're still here with me, and that's comforting enough for me, for now. So I guess I'll have to do the same with my gift, learn how to live with it, and if I need to cry to go for it.

I'm driving to the school, and I can't stop thinking about Lux, I can't stand him, but yet he's stuck in my head. I so badly want to hate him, which he doesn't make hard, but at the same time it seems like he means well for the most part. If I'm able to save people I'm going to, I don't care what he does. If he chooses to take me for saving people, then at least I saved some. That's what matters. I will keep saving people, even if it kills me.

I somehow make it to the school safe, I was so lost in my thoughts that I dissociated on the way here. I go to turn my car off when I'm hit with a premonition, and of course it is another person I know. How is it always someone I know when it's random like this? The first guy I bumped into I didn't know, and I was able to see his death right before. This is all still so strange, but I'm sure I'll get the hang of it soon. We do live in a small town, but I still don't know everyone here.

I see an office with a dark chestnut colored wooden desk, a nice office chair pushed into it, a laptop opened, and papers organized. The white shelf in the corner has books and random decor on it like a cactus. Mrs. Perri, the school counselor, walks in the room, duh it's her office, she's eating a muffin when she starts choking on it.

Fuck, how am I going to prevent her from choking on the muffin?! Saving people is not easy, I do know CPR if I don't make it to her in time. That's not guaranteed to work though. Also is death trying to mess with me? I get Mrs. Perri's job when she retires, and now she's about to choke. It's like death is trying to help Lux, and trying to get to the people they think I wouldn't save. Just because I'm next for her job, that doesn't mean I'm going to let her die. I am not that kind of person. I'm still going to do anything and everything I can to save her.

I quickly grab my bag from the passenger seat and my purple water bottle from the cupholder. I rush inside, throwing my keycard at the scanner with my lanyard attached, so it lets me in. I quickly set my bag under my desk, and rush down the hall to her office. The white walls, and lightly colored title floors of the hallways feel like they go on forever. Why is her office so far away from the school's office? It's almost at the back of the building, it might be a small town with a small school, but the building is still pretty large.

When I reach her office, she's actively choking. I attempt the heimlich maneuver on her, but it's not working.

"Someone help me!" I yell, as I'm still attempting to lift her up. She's not heavy, she's a small, thinner lady. I just can't seem to get this to work. Her face is becoming more pale, and her lips are starting to turn purple. Oh my gosh, I won't be able to do CPR on her if I can't get this out of her airway. Someone rushes in, I don't see who but they take over, and are able to get the chunk of muffin out of her airway. Mrs. Perri coughs a lot, but that's a good sign. She's breathing. Next thing I know, paramedics are moving around me to get to her. Everything is a blur.

"Sage? Are you okay?" Someone asks from beside me. My vision is becoming more blurry. I find the wall behind me, and sink down it with my back against it. Why am I so lightheaded? That's when everything goes black.

I'm only out for a few minutes, because I'm still sitting on the floor of Mrs. Perri's office. Principal Owens is sitting diagonally from me.

"Sage?" He asks.

"Is Mrs. Perri okay?" He nods a quick yes.

"I'm more worried about you right now. She's conscious and breathing. She's also on the way to the hospital to make sure all of it is out of her airway. Are you okay?"

"I think so. I don't know what happened."

"The paramedics think you stressed yourself out to the point of passing out. Your blood pressure was a little high, but nothing they were concerned about. I think you should take the day off. Go home, get some rest and come back tomorrow if you feel up to it. Don't force yourself though, if you need one extra day please don't feel like it won't be okay. We can handle the front office, but it might be a mess when you get back." He laughs. I smile at him.

"If it wasn't, then I'd run out of stuff to do pretty early in the day." I joke. He laughs again, before helping me up. "Thank you. I'll text you later today, and let you know how I'm feeling so I can give you enough notice for tomorrow just in case." I start walking out of Mrs. Perri's office.

"Only if you feel up to it!" He yells at me pointing at me.

"You got it!" I slowly head to the front office to grab my stuff. I don't want to walk too fast and get lightheaded again. I grab my bag, water bottle, and keys again. I head out to my car, as soon as I sit in the driver seat I lay my head back and close my eyes. What the hell just happened? I sigh, I guess this is my sign to go home and sleep the day away.

On my drive home, the events of this morning replay. Two mornings in a row. These are happening closer together. I don't know how I am going to be able to work with this new gift. Halfway during my drive home, I make a detour to my grandma and mom's house. They should be home, my mom works from home and Grams is retired.

I don't bother knocking, I just walk right in when I get there. Grams is sitting in her chair watching some soap opera on the tv. She looks up at me, surprised. My eyes well with tears, I didn't realize how upset I was until I actually looked at someone and saw concern on their face. I didn't even look at Principal Owens earlier, not directly. She stands up and pulls me into a hug.

"Aw sweetie, what's wrong? Tell me what happened." She says, before ushering me to the couch. We both sit on the couch and face each other.

"This 'gift' is hard. I've been able to save every person I've seen in a premonition so far. What if I can't save one? What if Lux really does come after me for messing up his job?" I talk fast with tears slipping down my cheeks.

"They can take time to get used to. Yours is unique, but it is a gift. Like you said, you've been able to save everyone you've seen so far. That's good! You won't be able to save everyone and sweetpea, that's okay." She comforts me and strokes my hair.

"I know, but Lux hates me because I keep saving the people he is supposed to reap."

"He will get over it, and will find others to reap in other cities, or states."

"That's just it. He won't get over it. He said he could just reap me out of nowhere if I keep getting in the way."

"Honey. Look at me." I look up at her, tears still streaming down my face. I'm so emotional, I must be about to start my period. "He is not going to reap you. Trust me."

"What makes you so sure?" I ask, throwing my hands up.

"I know you don't remember the day we almost lost you, but the day he saw you, the day we begged him not to take you from us, he was drawn to you."

"He said that to me too. Last night, he came over out of the blue." I fill her in on the events of last night. "I don't understand what he means by that." Grams laughs.

"Oh sweetie. He likes you. He has liked you since the day he met you. He wants to get to know you. Heck by now, the man probably loves you."

"How can you love someone you've only met a few times?"

"The heart always knows what it wants." She shrugs. "Your grandpa and I knew we loved each other after just a couple weeks, we were together for forty years, and I will never love again." We both smile.

"I miss him." I say, looking up at her again.

"Me too." She pulls me into a hug. "Now stop fighting this man or keep it up and just sleep together."

"Grams!" She laughs.

"I can't tell you how to live your life but go with the flow. The universe has a plan for you and knows which way to send you. Let the universe take the wheel if you need to. Listen to that great intuition of yours!"

"Yeah, you're right. I swear I say that at least once every time I am over here." I laugh, she is always right it seems, but she is my grandma and she has had more time on this Earth, so she knows a lot more than I do.

I spend the next few hours watching TV with her while my mom works in her office.

Chapter Five

The crisp Novemeber air is a little on the cooler side. The wind blows leaves around the streets in our small downtown area. The roads and streets aren't busy, but they aren't empty. You can hear the occasional honking, or the 'wait' when someone hits the crosswalk button. A woman with long dark red hair is blowing in the wind. She looks like she's in her early forties. She hits the crosswalk button at the main four-way intersection. The flashing hand signalling pedestrians not to walk turns to the walk symbol. She takes a few steps into the crosswalk when the asphalt below her gives out. A sinkhole the size of a SUV appears from where she was standing. She drops into the sinkhole. It's not only large, but it's deep. There's no way she can survive a fall from that height.

I take a deep breath in, taking in my actual surroundings. I'm still at the coffee shop downtown with my mom. Her dirty blonde hair, a little darker than mine, is pulled up in a hair tie. Her bangs out, and pushed to the side. She's taking a drink of her coffee when I come out of my premonition. She looks up at me with concern when I breathe in so deep.

"Are you okay, sweetie?" My mom asks. I stand up quickly. I don't bother grabbing my things.

"No, I'll be right back." I turn around, I move around all the table and chairs in the coffee shop before running out the doors. I stop to look to my right when I see the walk symbol for this block I take off in a run again. My premonition is only a couple blocks from here. I have to make it in time. I'm able to run through every crosswalk on my way to the woman. It's like the universe's way of saying that this lady needs to be saved.

When I get to the four-way that my premonition showed, I look for the redhead. She's nowhere in sight. The road where the sinkhole is going to appear is still intact. There has to be something I can throw on it to make the sinkhole appear before she gets here. If I can't find something, I'll have to grab her out of the way. She did look fragile, like she's battling an illness or she's just overcoming it.

I don't see anything that would be able to help me. Fuck, okay. It's going to be plan B. I can do this. I will not let her fall. I'm so scared, this needs to work. I suck in another deep breath when I see her coming up on the crosswalk.

I can do this. My heart is racing so hard, I can hear it in my ears and in my head. I've saved before before this, I can do it again. I am strong. I need to focus, but it's hard to concentrate when all I can hear is my heart beating.

She's at the crosswalk pole now. It's now or never. She hits the crosswalk button, waiting for the signal. Just as the light changes, telling her she can walk, I grab her arm and pull her back. A car pulls up to the crosswalk to turn right onto the next street, as the the sinkhole appears. Part of their car starts to fall into it, their back tires still on the solid asphalt. I hurry to the passenger door, and open it.

"You need to get out of the car right now," I say to the woman. I look towards the backseat to see a carseat. I open the backdoor as she gets out of the front seat. Right as I grab the carseat out of the car, her blue toyota falls into the sink hole. She breaks into a sob as I hand her the carseat with a newborn in it.

"Thank you," she manages to get out between sobs. I nod. Someone already made a call to the fire department. Police cars, firetrucks and ambulances are now blocking the street and the sinkhole.

"Thank you for saving my life." The redhead from my premonition says. She's standing beside me, and I almost jumped from not seeing her there. "I was just told this morning I was in remission. I'm officially cancer free." She smiles up at me. She has to be five foot, and now that we are closer, I can tell her red hair is a gorgeous wig. It suits her face. Her green eyes start to fill with tears.

She just got good news that she was in remission, and then she almost died from a sinkhole. That would have been so devastating for her family.

"I'm so happy that I was at the right place at the right time. Now go celebrate with family and friends. You deserve many more years." I say to her. She pulls me in for a quick hug which surprises me.

I hug her back before letting her go. Lux is standing behind her, looking directly at me. Oh goodness, here we go, *again.*

He walks up to me, and I so badly want to turn around. I really don't want to deal with his shit. I frown.

"Hey, job thief." Lux says, with a smirk on his face. Ugh, I so badly want to smack it right off his perfect face. I roll my eyes at him.

"Saving people is not 'job thieving.' Why can't you just leave me alone?"

"It is thieving, because I was suppose to reap them." I roll my eyes at him again. "If you keep rolling your eyes at me, darling, they're going to get stuck back there." I, so badly, want to roll my eyes again.

"Are we done here? I'd like to go back to what I was doing before this."

"Job thieving?"

"No, having coffee with my mom." He really likes to make everything about him.

"You'll have to tell her I say hi." He says, smirking again.

"No, thanks." I say, turning around to head back to the coffee shop I left my mom at.

"Stop saving the people I'm supposed to reap." He growls at me.

"Again, no thanks." He grabs my wrist and forces me to face him. I pull my wrist from his hand, a little too hard, because my wrist pops.

"For both of our sakes, stop interfering." He growls, again.

"I get the premonitions for a reason. Like I said twice already. No. Thanks." I say them separate this time, so maybe he will actually get the hint.

"You only get them, because you're a witch."

"A witch that's meant to save people." He rolls his eyes. "I was given this gift for a purpose."

"I'm done arguing with you. I'm not going to stop telling you to stay out of my way." His eyes look evil. As I go to say something back in retaliation, he disappears. Ugh, men suck. I turn back around to head back to the coffee shop.

"Is everything okay?" My mom asks, as I sit back down at our table. "I ordered you a fresh coffee. You didn't get to drink much of the other one, and it got cold while you were gone."

"Thank you, mom. I had another vision, and I had to go save her." My eyes start to fill with tears, it was a close call between the mother and her newborn baby, and the redhead. I'm starting to think that this gift won't get any easier, but hopefully I'll get more use to it. "I was able to save the women from my premonition, and two others. I also saved a new mother, and her newborn baby. A newborn almost died. The women I saw in my premonition that I saved first, she just found out she was in remission." I take a deep breath as a few tears escape from my eyes, and fall down my cheeks.

"Oh honey." My mom says, as she stands up to move to my side of the table. She gives me a side hug.

"She just survived cancer, and almost died by a sinkhole." I start to cry a little more. I'm so embarrassed. We are in a public place, and I'm crying like crazy. My mom doesn't seem to care if people are watching us, she just holds me from my side.

"You did a wonderful thing, sweetheart. You saved them, now they can enjoy more time with their families. You gave that newborn so much more time."

"I hope so."

We stay in the coffee shop a little longer, chatting about anything other than what I went through this morning. My mom is so easy to talk to when I need someone to just listen.

•.• •.•

Clara and Millie have been home for a couple weeks now, they ended up staying with family longer than they had originally planned. It was definitely getting lonely here without them. They want to have another party tonight, but I'm not sure I feel up to it, so I might just go hang out with my mom and Grams. I've been going over there at least once a week since my birthday. They have been even more amazing since I found out about my gift. My friends have also been helpful.

I can't make up my mind on if I want to stay for the party, or if I want to go hang out with my family. I do need a night to just let loose and enjoy myself after the last month I've had.

"Saaage!" Clara drags out my name, as she throws my door open, almost hitting the wall with it.

"Whaaat?" I look over at her from my desk. I've been sitting here lost in thought that I forgot I was writing in my journal.

"You have to stay and party with us tonight. We haven't had one since your birthday. Please." She gives me puppy dog eyes, and begs until I finally say yes. "Yay! You're the best, and I promise you won't regret it." She skips out of my room to go tell Millie. My phone buzzes, it's sitting beside my journal. I grab it, and check the notification.

Unknown Number: You seriously need to stay out of my way. I'm not going to keep telling you.

Me: Who is this?

Unknown Number: Oh please, don't act like you don't know. 😑

Me: I don't?

Unknown Number: Ohh I see, so you have a lot of people telling you to stay out of their way then?

Me: No...

Me: Oh. This is Lux isn't it?

Unknown Number: Ding Ding Ding, someone give the lady a prize.

Me: You sound stupid, it's just us two in the chat, that comment doesn't make any sense.

Lux: Whatever. Just do what I say.
Me: I'll do whatever the fuck I want.
Lux: You're going to regret it.

I can't help but roll my eyes as I set my phone down on my desk where it was before. Now I'm glad I told Clara I would stay for the party. I can't believe he had the nerve to text me. Wait, how did he even get my number?!

Me: How the fuck did you get my number?!
Lux: I have my ways darling.
Me: Don't call me that, it's weird. Seriously, how did you get my number?
Lux: I asked your grandma.

She didn't.

Me: She wouldn't do that.
Lux: Call and ask her, cause she did. Also it's not weird if you like it 😉

I don't respond to him, he doesn't need his ego fed anymore, if that's what we want to call it. I find the contact labeled 'Grams' and call her. I keep telling myself she wouldn't do that.

"Hello?" Grams answers the phone before the second ring.

"Grams, I don't think you did this, but I have to ask. Did you give Lux my phone number?" I rub my head with the hand not holding my phone while squeezing my eyes shut.

"Yep, I did." She pops her p. I sigh.

"Grams, why would you do that?" My voice is a little whiny.

"I can't tell you." I want to pull my hair out. Why is she being like this right now?

"Why can't you tell me? Grams, seriously I told you a couple weeks ago that he wants to reap me if I keep saving the ones he is supposed to reap." I hear her sigh on the other side of the phone.

"I shouldn't be telling you this, but your grandpa came to me in a dream last night. He told me someone was going to ask me for your phone number, and that I'm supposed to give it to them. He wouldn't tell me anything else."

"Ugh, darn it, Gramps. Promise that's all he told you?"

"Oh he also said he loves us all." My eyes start to tear up, but I push back the tears.

"Okay. Thanks Grams, that's all I needed."

"You aren't mad, are you?"

"No, just confused with that message from Gramps, and annoyed with Lux."

"It'll all reveal itself later, whatever Gramps meant."

"I hope so. I love you Grams, and I hope you have a good night."

"I love you too sweetie. Bye." We hang up, and I just sit there with my head in my hands for a few minutes. I need to process this. These damn gifts, mine, grams', my mom's. Ugh. They sometimes feel more like a curse. I'm getting drunk tonight now. I need to forget all of this for a bit.

"Clara, what time does the party start?" I yell from my desk hoping she's in the living room.

"In less than two hours." She yells back. It's a little past six now, so it sounds like the party is starting at eight. She could have just said eight.

I need to figure out what I'm going to wear tonight. A part of me wants to look good just in case one of my old flings shows up, and then another part of me just wants to wear my pajamas and get drunk.

I look through my closet, if nothing stands out to me, I'll wear pajamas. A purple floral dress? No. A mint green skin tight silk dress? No, too formal. That's when I see it, my constellation crop tank top. It's black and has iridescent constellations on it. It does show my boobs a little more than most of the other clothes I own, but I'm not going to care tonight. I pair the tank top with a pair of ripped black shorts.

I'll stick to my normal black eyeliner, and mascara for make up. Once I'm ready, I head out to the kitchen to help Clara and Millie. They have a bunch of bowls set out, and a couple inflatables for ice and drinks set up on the counters and the island. I open some of the bags of chips to pour into the bowls. Millie and Clara fill the inflatables with ice, before adding sodas, beers, wine coolers, and some other drinks in the ice.

"Is your Mr. Dreamy coming tonight?" Clara asks, winking at me. I laugh in disgust.

"As far as I know, he's not. He is not my Mr. Dreamy either. I can't stand him, and he can't stand me." Clara and Millie both laugh.

"Honey, that man might pretend to hate you when he's around you and to you, but I promise you that he doesn't." Millie says, shaking her head.

"She's right." Clara interjects, before I can say what I want to.

"Why does everyone insist he doesn't hate me? Even Grams says he doesn't, but you guys don't see how he is when I'm saving someone he is supposed to reap."

"Sure, he might be irritated or angry about that, but he does not hate you." Clara says, and Millie agrees.

"I'll believe it when I see it. He has threatened me a few times now, saying he'll reap me if I keep getting in the way." This causes the girls to burst out laughing again. "What now?"

"Sweetie, he says that to get you to back off. Judging by the way he looks at you, he wouldn't reap you." Clara says, adding more cans to the ice bath.

"Yeah, I guess we will just have to see because I'm not done saving people."

We finish getting things ready for the party. I go into my bedroom to check my makeup, and outfit one last time before people start flooding in. Hopefully tonight will be fun, and I won't get a premonition. It's been two days since my last one. They haven't been as frequent, but I'm not liking how spaced out they've been. I also don't want one every single day or multiple a day. I'm fine with this every few days, but it just makes me nervous. I don't want to get one tonight when I want to let loose. It's going to be a fun night.

✿ ✿

The party has been going on for over an hour now, and I'm on my first drink still. I decided to pace myself, because my gut is telling me I'm going to get a premonition tonight and I can't be wasted if there is someone I need to save. I could just be paranoid, and be overthinking which is most likely the case, but it's just a waiting game. Clara and Millie have been dancing together for the last twenty minutes, but you can see Clara is getting tired. We make eye contact, and I smile at her. She smiles back while making her way over to me. She plops down on the couch beside me, nudging me with her elbow, and that's when it happens.

Clara is talking to the DJ, when he suddenly trips on the cord by accident. She bends down to pick it up and plug it in, but as she's plugging it back in she gets electrocuted. It looks like her whole body shakes from it, and she's holding it like she can't let go of it until her body falls limp to the ground beside the DJ stand.

Oh shit, not my best friend, this could happen at any point tonight. I can't tell her about it, because she's wasted and would laugh. I'll have to keep a close eye on her tonight. Fuck, I need to pee, of course I need to now. Clara is staring off into space beside me, she's drunk alright.

"Alright come on, we need to find Millie." I say standing up and reaching my hand out. Please grab it. She looks up at me and grabs my hand.

"Ooo yes, lets find my beautiful wife." She giggles at her own comment. I don't bother correcting her. We find Millie in the crowd.

"Can you keep an eye on her for like five minutes?" I ask Millie. She nods, and says a quick 'of course' before they start dancing again. I make my way to the bathroom, do my business, and as soon as I start washing my hands I hear the speakers stop and multiple screams. Fuck fuck fuck. I should have told Millie about my premonition, I had to pee really bad, and didn't want to scare her. I hope they will understand. I run out of the bathroom, and I see the DJ with a blanket in his hands that was on the couch some feet away. He used it to pull Clara's hand from the speaker cord.

"Is she breathing? Someone fucking tell me she's breathing." Millie yells. I run to Clara's side and feel her pulse.

"It's very faint." I say looking up at Millie.

"There's an ambulance on the way." Someone from behind me says.

It feels like an eternity before the ambulance gets here, when they do they immediately check her pulse and get her on the gurney. Everyone has left the house, Millie yelled until everyone finally got the memo and left. Some were entertained, and wanted to stay just to watch. Disgusting. Millie rides to the hospital in the ambulance with Clara, and I follow in my car.

We get to the hospital in less than ten minutes, and they take Clara back to a room. They aren't allowing Millie or I back there with her right now.

"She flatlined in the ambulance." Millie says her voice breaking, and tears start to flow. "I-I don't know if they got her back or not... I-I don't know..." I pull her into a hug.

"She's where she needs to be. They can help her, they will bring her back." She nods, still crying. I know that she won't be able to talk without crying uncontrollably, that's how I get. I'm starting to cry too, I need my best friend here with me. We sit in the lobby, crying and blowing our noses. Two hours later, we get called back to Clara's room.

"Clara suffered some burns on her hand from the electrocution. It also messed with her heart's rhythm. We will need to monitor her for at least twenty-four hours, if not longer. As of right now, she's going to be fine." The doctor tells us once we reach her room.

"Thank you doctor. Can I stay overnight with her?" Millie asks.

"Of course, no more than two visitors at a time out of visiting hours, so you both can stay overnight if you wish." We nod, and thank him one more time. He leaves the room.

"Do you want me to run home quickly for pajamas for you?" I ask Millie, she's already sitting in the chair beside Clara holding her hand that didn't get burned.

"No, it's fine I can sleep in this."

"Are you sure? It's really not a problem." She nods.

"Thank you though. Are you going to stay the night up here?" She asks, looking at me.

"Do you want me to? I won't if you want to be alone with her. I understand."

"You can stay a couple hours, but you should go home and sleep comfortably." She says, looking back at Clara.

"Okay, I'm going to go find a drink. Do you want anything?" She shakes her head no. I slip out of the room quietly. I see something that looks awfully like a grim reaper's robe out of the corner of my eye. I look in the direction to see Lux in his work uniform, motioning me to come to the janitor's closet.

I so badly want to turn and go the opposite direction, but I feel this magnetic pull pulling me towards the closet. I make sure no one is around when I go in, and close the door. There is one little light on the ceiling, this is one creepy closet.

"What could you possibly want? My best friend almost fucking died tonight, actually she did for at least a minute." I whisper-yell at Lux. He steps closer to me, this closet is tiny, and it's only getting smaller. I back up with each step he takes towards me until I'm against the wall, and standing next to a rack with cleaning supplies on it. He puts one hand on the wall beside my head, and the other on my throat. He doesn't squeeze, he simply just holds my throat. Oh shit, he's going to kill me.

"You have no idea what you keep doing." His voice is like a low growl.

"I do know what I'm doing, I'm saving people." I manage to squeak out, just because I'm nervous from how close he is to me, and I feel like he could snap my neck at any time. He tilts my head to the side, before his mouth collides with the skin of my neck, his hand doesn't leave my throat as he sucks on a part of my neck above his hand. I can't help but let out a little moan. "You really piss me off."

"Better to be pissed off than pissed on." I say, smirking.

"Oh you think you're funny, huh?"

"I like to think so, yeah." I say shrugging. His lips collide with mine, the kiss becomes heated quickly. He lets go of my throat, and he takes my tank top off. I help him get his robe off, before forcing his lips back onto mine. He's only in boxers now, and I still have everything but my tank top on. He definitely exercises, but doesn't quite have a six pack, and he's not skinny.

He's perfect. He unclasps my bra, as our make out session continues. He takes one of my C cup breasts into his hand, before trailing kisses down my jaw and taking the other into his mouth. I suck in a breath, I haven't had any guy make me feel this good just by the foreplay, in a while, actually now that I think about it, ever. No guy has made me feel this good. He removes my pants, and my underwear before taking his own off. His penis flops out effortlessly, almost like it needs and wants this as much as I do right now. I despise this guy, but fuck he is making me feel things I never thought I could. He lifts me onto a small table in the closet that once had more cleaning supplies on it before he set me down.

He drops to his knees before kissing my inner thighs, I suck in another breath. He finds my clit easily with his thumb, he rubs it in circular motions just how I like. He rubs faster and faster, causing me to moan. He lifts his other hand to cover my mouth.

"Shh darling. We don't want to get caught, do we?" I shake my head, no. "Good girl, now let me taste you." He replaces his thumb with his tongue, swirling it around my clit and sucking every now and then.

He keeps my mouth and moans covered with his hand. Fuck this feels good. My legs start to shake as I orgasm. He pulls his mouth away from between my legs. He grabs a condom from the box sitting on the shelf of extra medical supplies. He wraps his dick with it, before placing it at my entrance.

"Are you okay with this?"

"I don't like you, but I like this and need this, so yes I'm okay with what we are doing. Now will you shut up and just fuck me?"

"Damn, darling."

"I said shut up." He laughs, and slowly pushes his throbbing dick into my wet core. I suck in another breath, and let out a soft moan. Yeah, I really needed this, a release. I can't believe it is with this psycho though. His thrusts pick up in pace, and his thumb finds my clit again. Double the pleasure, this man really knows what he is doing. I'm going to finish again in no time. His thumb rubs faster, as he picks up his pace. He lets out a few moans of his own.

"Holy shit, I might not like you either, but you feel so good." He whispers in my ear.

"That makes two of us." I whisper back. He moves his head back to continue how hard and fast he's going. His thrusts pick up, a few things fall from the shelves beside us. We both looking over at what fell, and back at each other. We laugh, but he pushes deep into me, he hits my cervix a little and I wince in pain a little. He mumbles a quick sorry, before adjusting his pace. We both finish together, before crashing our lips together once more.

"This can never happen again." He says, holding my cheek with his hand and looking me in the eyes. His face is so close to mine, and I so badly want to kiss those soft lips more.

"Never again." I agree, before standing and forcing him out of my way without actually touching him. We get dressed without saying another word, I head to find the nearest bathroom to clean up. I've already been gone longer than I should have been so Millie is definitely going to question me when I get back into Clara's room. After cleaning up quickly in the bathroom, I find a vending machine and buy a can of Coca-Cola and an orange cream soda for Millie. I head back to the room, and slip in as a nurse leaves.

"Did you get lost? You were gone for over a half hour." Millie says, still looking down at her phone.

"I saw an old friend in the hallway, and they decided they wanted to catch up right then and there. I had to use the bathroom as my escape to get back here. I didn't want them to think I didn't actually have to go, so I went then I went and found the sodas."

"I didn't need the whole story. I believe you. Was it a guy?" She laughs and looks up at me.

"Yeah, someone I knew from high school."

"Did he know Clara?"

"No, he went to a different school. Him and I met up a few times in high school to mess around." I say, looking down at the can of Coke in my hands. I open it, and take a sip as Millie does the same with her drink.

"Did you sleep with him?" She asks, and I almost spit out my drink.

"Here? Hell no." I can feel my face heating up.

"In high school." She laughs again.

"That's what messing around means." I say, laughing. She shakes her head at me as she laughs. She turns her attention back to her phone. I set my drink down on the bedside table beside Clara's bed before pulling the folding chair out of the closet.

"I'll hang out for a little longer, and then I'll head home. If you need anything from home that you want me to bring up tomorrow just let me know." I say, before pulling out my phone to scroll my social media.

"Thanks." Millie says. We stay quiet for the rest of the time I'm there. Nurses come into Clara's room every half hour to make sure her vitals are good. After an hour of endless scrolling on my phone, and watching some tv, I tell Millie I'm going to head home. She gives me a quick hug before I leave. I leave a small kiss on Clara's head. I head to the parking garage, but feel someone following me. I don't bother turning around, but I stop midway through the garage, I'm almost to my car. I could just try to run to my car, but his teleporting ass can just teleport right in front of me before I can jump in.

"Why are you following me?" I ask the man standing behind me. "Missing me already?"

"Nah I've had better." Ouch.

"So again, why are you following me?"

"Just want to make sure you get to your car safely."

"Sure, that's it. You want to be nice to me for once. I highly doubt that." I start walking to my car again.

"I'm just trying to look out for you." He says, sighing.

"Why do you want to look out for me? We don't even like each other." I stop, and turn around to face him. My arms are in the air now, at my sides but stretched out.

"No we don't, because you are a pain in the ass who likes to get in my way constantly."

"Exactly why this is so confusing. I can't take this anymore." I drop my arms to my side and shake my head.

"Do what anymore?"

"These mixed signals you are always giving me. One minute you act like maybe you want to be around me, which is shocking, and then the next you're back to being a dick who claims he hates me."

"Oh darling, I don't hate you."

"Well you act like it. It's getting late, can I please go home now?" I say before pointing to my car that I'm now standing next to. I want to be far from this man. "If you want to dislike me, or whatever you want to call it, then stick to that. Don't switch up when you feel like it, I'm sick of men thinking they can just toy with my feelings all the time. I do not deserve that! If you want to be friendly, then do that. Stick to one for fucks sake." He looks a little shocked, like he didn't expect me to snap at him this way, but it's all true. I'm sick of thinking he can play these mind games with me every time he sees me. He doesn't say anything before nodding. He turns around and leaves. I didn't think he'd make it that easy but okay. I want to watch him go, but I don't, instead I get in my car and drive home.

Chapter Six

Clara is recovering well, it's been two days since the accident happened. The doctors are discharging her today, Millie is thrilled. I haven't seen Lux since Friday night in the the parking garage. I should be happy about that, but all I can think about is the time we spent in the storage closet. A part of me regrets it, while another part of me wants to experience his touch again. He's not just frustrating when he gets mad at me for saving the people he needs to reap, but also in the way that I'm now craving, yearning for his touch. It's so wrong to feel this way. I still can't stand him. I think of the way his thumb rubbed my clit as he was deep inside me, my legs were shaking from pleasure. I shake my head, trying to get these thoughts out.

"Hey space cadet, are you going to come back down to Earth?" Clara says from beside me, sitting on the side of her hospital bed. I look up over at her and smile.

"Sorry, my mind is all over the place." Millie went to go get some sodas for us while we wait for the discharge papers.

"It's okay, what's going on?"

"Just the same shit with Lux." She nods, in understanding.

"Anything new that I've missed with your little feud?"

"Uh yeah, about that..." I pause, I have to tell her. She's my best friend and would kill me if I didn't tell her. "We had sex."

"What?!" She practically yells.

"Shhh I didn't tell Millie." She gives me a look like I'm messing with her.

"Haven't told me what?" Millie says entering Clara's room. I sigh.

"Alright well it looks like I'm telling you what actually happened Friday night." I tell them about the events of Friday night after we got here. I don't tell them the details cause knowing them they don't want to hear all of that.

"You did it where?!" Clara exclaims.

"The closet down the hall, like I said at the beginning."

"Yeah, I heard you the first time. I just needed to hear where again." She says before pausing. She whispers the next two words. "The hospital." She shakes her head, and grins.

"What is that face for?"

"You fucking go girl, that's awesome!" Clara says, still super excited.

"I mean the sex was awesome, sure, but it happening with him that was not awesome. It shouldn't have happened, and I still don't like him." I say shaking my head.

"Oh come on, if it was the best sex you ever experienced, you should put that hate into the sex and get over it. Find a way to like each other and gain each other's trust." Millie says. The nurse comes in, and thankfully we get distracted by

Clara's discharge process, so I don't have to continue this conversation. He doesn't deserve to earn my trust after the threats, and acting the way he does. I head downstairs to go get my car pulled up to the patient pick up area, while Clara and Millie finish going through the discharge area and signing the paperwork. I park my car in the space reserved for patient pick up, and wait. I glance at my phone to see no notifications. I look back up at the hospital doors, they still aren't on their way out.

"Hey." A voice says from my backseat. I jump, and turn around.

"How the fuck did you get in here without opening or closing the doors?!" I ask, my voice full of anger.

"I can pretty much teleport wherever I want to." Lux says, shrugging.

"So you think it's okay to just teleport into someone's car without any warning?"

"Well, when it's your car, yes." He smirks.

"Don't you have people's souls you need to reap?" He shrugs again, which makes me roll my eyes.

"You are so infuriating. I asked you to stop with these mind games."

"You didn't ask, you yelled at me."

"That was my way of asking. I'm going to end up murdering you before you get the chance to do it to me if you keep this shit up." I say, shaking my head and turning back around in my seat to face the steering wheel.

"You can't murder me, love. I'm immortal."

"Fine, I'll just lock you in my basement in a chair within a pentagram and torture you for the rest of my life. You can't do anything stuck in a pentagram, and without your scythe."

"You forgot one thing."

"What's that?"

"I can teleport, not in a pentagram no, but you're going to have a hard time catching me." His words make him smirk again.

"Oh, I will find a way, it's not only a threat, its a promise."

"Ooo sounds kinky." I see him wink from the rearview mirror, I want to vomit.

"You're disgusting."

"Mm I don't think so, you enjoyed me the other night, if I remember correctly."

"Is there something you need? Why are you doing this shit again?" Lux shrugs again.

"I was bored, and you are easy to mess with."

"I'm trying to pick my friend up from the hospital, can you just leave me alone please?"

"Ohh she's asking nicely this time." He says to literally no one. I turn to face him again and shoot him a glare. "Fine fine, I have someone I need to go reap now anyway." He disappears, and I turn back in my seat to see Clara being wheeled out in the wheelchair with a nuse pushing her, Millie by her side.

Lux ruined my entire mood, but seeing Clara on her way to my car brings some of the happiness back. It'll be nice to have my best friend back in the house. I hate when they are gone, it's too quiet in the house when they aren't there. Clara climbs into the passenger seat, Millie gets in the backseat with Clara's bag of belongings and her discharge instructions.

"I'm glad you're coming home." I say, looking over at Clara. She smiles.

"Me too." She grabs my hand and squeezes before putting it behind her to hold Millies hand. We head home in comfortable silence.

•.• •.•

Clara and Millie have been resting in their room since we got home around noon. They are both exhausted from not getting great rest at the hospital. I decide to go to the park for a bit, swings have always helped me relax. I make sure I have my earbuds, and my phone when I head out the door. Once I'm at the park, I put my earbuds in, turn on my favorite playlist, and start swinging on the swing set. The November air is a little chilly even with my sweater and sweatpants on. I don't mind it, the air also smells crisp, and a little like pollen. I'm surprised it's still sixty degrees out, and still no snow yet in sight. I'm not complaining though, I hate the snow, but this is crazy for the midwest.

I swing for a half hour before I notice someone on the swing next to me. They must have gotten on the swing when I was up in the air and couldn't see them. They are also facing the other way, I go backwards in the air and so do they. Of

75

course, it's Lux. I slow my swinging down, and allow it to come to a stop on it's own. I want to get off and walk away before he has the chance to say anything, but I also can't move. My head is what's yelling at me to get up, and go home, but it's my heart telling me to stay, to hear him out. I'm so sick of him just appearing. He knows that, and does it just to drive me crazy. I sigh, sitting on my swing, no longer pushing myself. I pull my earbuds out, and put them back in their case.

"What do you want now?" I ask, looking over at him, his swing is now stopped to and he is already looking at me.

"I never told you what I came to tell you earlier in your car." Lux says, not looking away from me.

"What's that?" I look forward at the pond about twenty feet away.

"I'm sorry for the way I acted in the parking garage. I don't mean to give you mixed signals, honestly. I've tried to explain this to you before but you still don't seem to understand it. I've said it before and I will say it again. I'm drawn to you, but you mess with my job by saving those around you in this little town. I want to act on those feelings like I did the other night in the closet at the hospital, but falling for you, for any mortal that isn't another reaper is forbidden." He goes to continue but I hold up my hand, making him stop before saying whatever he was going to.

"Hold on. You are drawn to me, you want to act on the said feelings you have, but you told me in quote, 'I've had better' in the parking garage after the incident in the closet. Make that make sense to me." I say looking at him again.

"I lied. Okay?!" He yells. "I lied." He whispers this time.

"Why?" I whisper.

"I had to say that or I would have walked back up to you and kissed you again. I lied not only to you, but to myself. You were the best I've ever had, and I'm not just saying that to get you on my side or to get you to stop saving the people I need to reap." His eyes are showing his emotions now when usually I can't see how he's feeling through them. "I mean it."

"I just, I don't know if I can believe you." I look down at my hands.

"Look, I just want to get to know you better. I want to know your favorite foods, your favorite color, your favorite show, band, favorite everything. If we try to pursue something, we keep the whole you saving the people I'm suppose to reap out of the relationship. I get it, you see it happening in your visions, you feel the need to save them. You're empathic, and I'm not, but I understand as much as I can without being one." He stands before walking over to my swing. He puts his hands on the chains of my swing one on each chain. My knees and legs are between his as I'm still sitting on my swing.

"What makes you think I want to pursue something? Also, I thought you said it was forbidden." I'm still looking down at my hands, and his legs since they are right by my hands in my lap.

"It is forbidden, but I've never been one to follow rules. Will you look at me?" I keep my vision on my hands. "Sage." One of his hands let go off the swing chain to put it on my chin. He lifts up my chin to force me to look at him.

"What?" I say quietly, not letting my eyes meet his.

"Seriously look at me please." I don't think I have ever heard him say please, or if I have this is one of the very few times. I let my eyes meet his. He smiles. "There are those bright eyes I like so much." I roll my eyes, he's gotta be joking right now.

"You never answered my question." I say, my eyes not leaving his.

"I know. I'm trying to hide my hurt." He's not lying, his electrifying blue eyes show hurt.

"I just asked why you thought I'd want to pursue a relationship, that's not me rejecting you."

"Really? Cause your tone had said otherwise when you asked it." He still isn't removing his gaze from mine. The fall wind picks up, blowing leaves at and around us.

"I didn't have a tone. I was speaking normal." I shake my head, laughing. "I wasn't trying to hurt you, I was trying to rephrase the way you said it, but also ask seriously why you would think that. We don't like each other, and don't even get along." I look down again at my hands, at my black nail polish I put on the other night while I was home alone. It's already chipping away, so I pick at the polish more.

"We don't get along because you get in my way."

"I get in your way because those people deserve to live longer." He pushes back, and lets go of my swing.

"You don't even know anything about those people, how do you know they deserve to live longer?" His eyes now show anger instead of hurt.

"I don't care if I don't know them at all, they still deserve to live!" I'm fuming now, I push off my swing. "See this is exactly why we wouldn't work in a relationship. Fuck, we couldn't even be friends." I turn around, walk through the two swings we were just sitting in, and head home.

"Seriously, you say that and don't even give me a chance to say something back." He says, following me now.

"Oh sorry, I forgot, you usually prefer to get the last word in, don't you? You can always teleport in front of me, I'm surprised you didn't in the parking garage and now." I shake my head still walking. He's caught up with me now, right on my heels.

"I didn't want to argue anymore in the parking garage. Believe it or not, I don't like arguing with you." He says, walking in front of me causing me to stop. I roll my eyes, and turn my head to my left to avoid his gaze. I focus my attention on a tree that has a lot of orange, and red leaves. When the wind blows, some of leaves make their way to the ground. Leaves that are already on the ground, move around with the wind. "There you go not looking at me again."

"I have a hard time looking at people that I'm angry at."

"You're hardly ever going to look at me since you're always angry at me."

"Well, that brings me some happiness." It doesn't because I actually enjoy his face.

"Oh whatever. Please look at me. Again, I understand why you feel the need to save them. Let's just try to keep things separate." He puts his hand on my left cheek since I'm still looking towards the left, and he forces me to look at him. "We could keep our friendship, relationship, whatever you want to call it separate from what we do. I still reap, and attempt to reap the ones you save before you save them. No matter what, we don't let the saving and reaping get in the way of getting to know each other. If it doesn't work, then we go back to being enemies, easy."

"I'm not sure if that's easy, Lux."

"All of it, or the going back to enemies if it doesn't work out part?"

"All of it. Let's say we did get to know each other better, we formed a relationship, fell for each other and it didn't work out. If we both end up loving each other, it's going to be hard for us to be enemies again." I say, looking at him with his hand still on my cheek.

"That's just a risk we will have to take." He says, smirking.

"I'll think about it." I say, and he nods.

"That's fine, take all the time you need. I can wait another ten or so years." He says, smirking again, before winking. I can't help but smile a little, I can also feel my face get a little warm. "I'll talk to you later." He kisses my left cheek before removing his right hand from my cheek. He leaves, and I'm hit with a premonition.

It's the same guy from my first premonition, he was eating a meatball sub before having a heart attack. *The man is a bit on the heavier side, he is holding another sub sandwich at a sandwich shop. He experiences another heart attack the same way. I see the green booths, and tables which help me realize which sandwich shop it is. Jolly's Sub Shop.*

The sub shop is a five minute walk from the park I'm at, so I'm going to run and hope to get there in two minutes. If I remember right, the EMT's at the scene the first time he had a heart attack, they said he had diabetes and that he would be prone to another heart attack if he didn't watch his diet.

I make a run for the sub shop, and I do make it in two minutes, right as the man I've saved once before collapses. I rush into the shop, and attempt to preform CPR on him again. Lux shows up behind me in his reaper uniform, he puts his hand on my shoulder, I don't stop attempting CPR.

"Sage, it's not going to work." Lux says, softly. "You've already saved him once. People can only be saved once, even I can't bring him back." I can't help but start crying, I get up off the ground and run home. I lock my bedroom door, before flopping down onto my bed face down. I've saved everyone so far, this is the first person I couldn't save. Someone knocks on my bedroom door before trying the handle. I try to ignore it, and put a pillow on my head to allow myself to grieve. I didn't know the man, but I feel like I deserve to grieve, the man I tried to save that should have had a longer life. Another knock comes after a couple minutes.

"If you don't answer, I'm just going to just come in." Of course, it's Lux, again. I don't respond, or move from my bed. "I'm coming in." I hear behind my door a few minutes later. I feel his presence beside my bed.

"I'm sorry that you couldn't save him." He says as he sits on my bed beside me. I snuffle, and nod. He rubs my back, gently in soft circles.

"I just don't understand how this is fair?! Why wouldn't I save him again?" I say, moving the pillow off my head, but staying on my stomach, I turn my head to the left to face him, but I don't look at him.

"Those are unfortunately the rules, darling. You did what you could. It's okay if you don't save everyone, and I'm seriously not just saying that because then I can do my job properly. I actually kind of secretly like when you intervene, I look for you everytime now, but sometimes I forget you won't be at some of the deaths because they aren't nearby." I sniffle. Why am I such a crybaby?

"I know, but it's still sad. I'm such an emotional person, I'm sorry you're seeing me like this. Also, you look for me?"

"I do. I'm used to you showing up to save people. I hate that I have to snap at you, but I have to follow my job and my rules. It's okay to cry over the people you can't save, especially since he didn't have any family. That man deserves to mourned, and you are doing that." He says, wiping some of my tears away with his thumb. Lux blue eyes soften, the second time I've ever seen his eyes so soft, the icy blue glisten a little. Is he getting emotional now? "Will you sit up please? So I can hug you."

"I don't really want to move." I say before putting my face into my mattress.

"Alright, well if you don't want to sit up, then I'll just have to do this." I feel the bed dip more beside me, strong arms wrap around me, and pull from my stomach to my side. Lux is cuddling me, holding me in his big muscly arms. "Feel free to weep more if you need to."

"You're still in your reaper robes, I don't want to get your uniform wet with my tears." I say, rolling over to face him. His hood is down, and his blonde hair is messier than usual. It looks like he was repeatedly messing with it. A few more tears slip down my cheeks. He wipes them away again, his hand stays on my cheek, his thumb making the soft strokes that I love. Wait. What am I thinking? Love. No, it's just nice. I don't love it. I can't love it.

"It's okay if you get my uniform wet with tears. It'll dry, and I can always wash it. No big deal." His blue eyes don't leave my glossed over blue ones. He pulls me closer to him, and I cry more into his chest. Lux only moves his hand over

my hair trying to soothe me, and just holds me. He
smells of cologne, not death. I swore his uniform
would smell bad, and that he would smell more
awful after reaping, but he smells good. The scent is
earthlike, a mix of pine and sage, and a little hint of
smoke. Maybe he just lit some sage before
teleporting here. I pull my sky blue soft blanket,
over me, Lux's arms still around me. I fall asleep
with some tears still slipping down my cheeks.

Chapter Seven

I wake up to Lux being gone, and it's dark outside. It's after eleven. I'm not sure if I can get back to sleep now. I notice a figure standing in front of my door, I rub my eyes but it doesn't go away.

"Hello?" I ask. Not taking my eyes off of it now.

"Love," A deep slow voice says before pausing. "Is forbidden between a human and a reaper. You must not be romantically or physically involved. If this happens, you will be killed. He will be sentenced to the highest torture, and will no longer be allowed to reap. He will also be locked away for eternity since he can't die." With that, the figure disappears. What the fuck. Now I'm really not going to be able to go back to sleep. I sigh, before turning my tv, I need to watch my comfort movies after that. I grab my phone off my brown beside table. I put in the passcode, and open up the messaging app.

Me: I just had a really strange encounter.
Lux: Are you okay?
Me: I'm fine. Honestly a little shaken up, it was freaky.
Lux: Need me to come back over? I have two more people to reap, then I can come over.

Me: Uh, I'm not sure it's a good idea after that encounter, but you deserve to know about it so actually yes please.
Lux: Okay, give me like half an hour. Can I just teleport into your room?
Me: Yep, that's fine. Thank you for asking.

I put my phone down beside me, and turn my attention back to my tv. I'm not sure if horror is the right genre after what just happened, but I want to watch my favorite horror movie, *Scream*. So fuck it, that's what I'm going to do. Not long into the movie, Lux appears in my room right in front of my tv. I glare at him, which makes him realize he's in my way. He climbs onto my bed, turns on my lamp and sit's beside me, I move over giving him more room while also sitting up more.

"I haven't seen this movie in awhile. It's ironic that *Ghostface* is also known as the reaper, and I'm a reaper. I'd never murder anyone though, especially not like the way they do." Lux says, putting his arm around my shoulder.

"No, you just reap people after they've been murdered, or have just died." I try to move away from his arm around his shoulder. He notices, and moves it from behind him.

"What's wrong?" I sigh, and pause the movie.

"I woke up just a little after eleven, you were gone, but I noticed someone or something standing by my door. It was dark in here, so I couldn't see what they looked like. He had a deep voice and he talked slow. He said reapers and humans can't be together. If he catches us together, you will be sentenced to the highest torture, locked away for eternity, and you wouldn't be a reaper anymore. He also would kill me" I say, my eyes welling up with tears. I've cried so much today. He sighs, and looks at the paused movie on my tv.

"That was Death, my boss. I'd say he was just trying to scare you, but unfortunately he's serious. I've seen it before. He's not someone to mess with." He's still in his uniform, so he starts fidgeting the cloth.

"Oh." I don't know what else to say. He nods.

"He's a scary guy. The last reaper that fell in love with a human, got beat every single day, since we can't die, Death just kept switching out the guy that was torturing him. The only break he'd get from the beating was when he was locked in his cage. He tortures people for a total of two to three years, before putting them into the cage. You can't teleport when you're stuck in that chair being tortured, or when you're locked in the cage. It's terrifying. Do you know what's more terrifying though?" He tells me, before looking at me. I don't move my eyes from his.

"What's more terrifying than that?" I ask, his piercing blue eyes start to tear up. I can tell he wants to break eye contact but he's forcing himself to continue to look at me.

"It's terrifying to think about not getting to be with you. I need to be around you, I need to get

to know you more, I need to be with you." He says
as tears fall into his lap. "You drive me crazy
sometimes, but I would risk endless torture after
getting to be with you."

"I'm sorry, but I'm only twenty-five. I don't
want to die yet. I don't want to be killed by your
boss. We've only just started to tolerate each other
when I'm not stopping you from reaping." He nods.

"I-I understand." His voice cracks, and then
he's gone. I sigh heavily, I have a love hate
relationship with his teleportation ability. I want to
scream now, but instead I just go back to the movie.
I turn off my lamp, and lay down again. Eventually
I fall back asleep to the movie.

I sleep until almost ten, when I hear Clara
and Millie in the kitchen. I get up, throw my
lavender robe on over my sleep shirt, and
sweatpants. When I walk into the kitchen, they're
making waffles.

"Herb!!" Clara says, running over to me and
hugging me. I laugh.

"Well you are definitely back to your normal
self." I say to her. Millie agrees.

"We're making some waffles, if you'd like
some." Millie says. They both have flour on their
noses and cheeks. I'm assuming they had a playful
flour fight. Clara has her hair pulled back into a hair
tie, and Millie has her short black emo styled hair
down.

"Can I talk to you guys about something?" I ask them sitting down on the barstool of the island.

"If it's about Lux, than definitely." Clara says, before turning around to put more mix into the waffle maker. I sigh.

"Girl, you might be a psychic cause you're right."

"Well we knew he was here last night." Millie says, earning herself a hit on the arm from Clara. "What? I'm not going to lie to her."

"But she also lives here so she can have whoever she wants here." Clara says.

"I never said she couldn't." Millie argues. Clara sighs, and nods. She mumbles a quick 'sorry' to her fiance. Millie gives her a quick side hug.

"Okay, spill the piping hot tea." Clara says, looking at me again. I laugh again.

"It's honestly not that good. I fell asleep crying in his arms last night after I couldn't save that man from the mall again. Apparently, you can only save someone from being reaped once. It's the rules." I say shrugging. They are both looking at me intrigued. "Anyways, I woke up sometime after eleven to this creepy ass figure standing by my door." I go on to tell them about what Death said.

"That's terrifying." Clara and Millie say in unison.

"Yeah that's what I told Lux last night. I texted him, and he came back over. He said it's more terrifying not getting a chance to be with me, than being tortured for who knows how long because he fell for me. My life was also threatened

though, I'm only twenty-five. I still have a whole life
ahead of me. I want to get married, have kids, buy a
house of my own, watch you two get married and
raise kids. The works, ya know?" I say to them,
they're still staring at me. The waffle maker dings,
and Clara hurries up to take it out so she can face
me again. They both agree with me wanting the
whole shabang when it comes to life. "I told him I
just couldn't risk that. He said he understood, and
just teleported out of my room." I swear Millie and
Clara's jaws drop at the same time.

"He just left?" Clara asks.

"He didn't even try to fight for you?" Millie
asks.

"Yep, and he might think he's tried enough
already, because I've turned him down a few times.
I just don't think it would work out, we hardly get
along. I get in his way. It's forbidden to be together.
I just... I can't. Maybe I just need some more time."
I say shrugging.

"You're only getting older sweetie, time goes
by fast. Don't make him wait too long, because it'll
be less time he gets with you." Clara says. She
makes a good point, but he's immortal. Eventually,
there will come a time he is without me.

"There's going to be a time he's without me
again, I'll die at some point, hopefully when I'm
ninety, but he's immortal."

"Exactly why you should just give him a
chance. The worst that can happen is you'll get
caught and killed, but you were each other's
everything's until that point." Millie says. "I would

love to grow old with this, but if I died today, I'd be satisfied with the time we had together because she'll know I'll always love in the beyond and I'll know she'll always love me too." This makes Clara tear up a little.

"Aww, I agree." Clara says before they kiss.

"You guys are so cute it's disgusting." I say, laughing.

"We know, you tell us at least once a week." Clara says laughing.

"Listen to us, you don't want to regret not giving him a chance in five years when he's met someone new, or has a reaper wife or whoever the hell they are allowed to date." Millie says.

"Ugh, I hate that you two are right. How is tomorrow Monday already?" I say, changing the subject. They both shrug. We spend the rest of the morning eating waffles and talking about what they have planned for the wedding so far. I zone out a little to think about Lux, and what I'm going to do.

Chapter Eight

Clara and Millie decided to spend the day out in the town after we all had breakfast this morning. They invited me to go with, but I declined. I need to figure out what I'm going to do about Lux. My heart yearns for him. He's sweet when he isn't trying to reap, he's attractive, and those blue eyes. I could look into them forever. I'm about to make a huge risk right now.

> **Me:** Hey, can we talk about last night?
> **Lux:** I'm a little busy right now.
> **Me:** When will you be free?
> **Lux:** Not sure.
> **Me:** Oh. Okay..

That didn't go the way I had hoped. I sink lower into the couch cushions. Now what do I do? Wait for another premonition? They're so unpredictable, and random. Fuck it, I'm going to text him again. Geez, I sound like a girl obsessed over her ex.

> **Me:** Please let me know when you're free, or off work or whatever.
> **Lux:** 👍

Ugh, what an asshole. I can't help but roll my eyes. I need to burn off some steam. I'm

frustrated, and honestly I just want to slap him, but
also rip his clothes off at the same time. I head to
my room, to put on a sports bra and some leggings
but my phone buzzes before I have the chance to
change.

> **Lux:** I have one person left to reap on the
> West Coast, then I can come over. Is that
> okay?
> **Me:** 👍

I smirk to myself, I have to give him a taste
of his own medicine. I put my running clothes
away, I still want to get out of my lounging clothes
before he gets here. I can't be wearing the same
clothes as yesterday when he gets here. I quickly
put on a pair of black comfy shorts, and a black
tank top. I head back out to the living room, and
clean up my snack mess, which is just a bag of
popcorn and some cookies.

There's a knock at the door a few minutes
later, I open the door and I freeze. Lux is standing
there, and he isn't in his reaper uniform. He has a
tight mint green shirt, and skinny black jeans with
some ripped holes in them on. Hot damn. He looks
good, and holy crap it's chilly out today, maybe the
shorts and tank top was a bad move.

"Are you going to let me in or just gawk at
me forever?" Lux says, smirking. He's leaning
against the door, and I swear my heart skips.

"Yeah, sorry." I say, moving to the side so he
can come in. I'm so nervous.

"So what about last night did you want to talk to me about?" He asks before sitting down on the couch. I don't sit directly beside him, but just far enough away that I can face him.

"The way you just left first of all." My tone is frustrated.

"I didn't have anything else to say."

"But what if I did?!"

"You would've cut me off, or texted me right after I left."

"I had asked you to come over, I wasn't going to try to get you to come back over right away. You're so infuriating."

"I'm infuriating?! Me?!" He yells, standing and pacing. "No no, you got that all wrong. I've tried, I've expressed my feelings. I've told you I want to get to know you more, I am fucking drawn to you." He walks closer to me, he leans down in front of me, and puts his face close to mine.

"You truly have no idea how I feel towards you, darling. No fucking idea. I tell you I'm drawn to you. I tell you that I want to try something and you just keep pushing me away." He doesn't move.

"I-I'm sorry. I'm just scared." My voice comes out small.

"Scared of what?" He whispers.

"Your boss for one. I want to get married, have kids, buy a house, grow old, the whole life experience. I can't do that if we get together and your boss finds out." I say, causing him to sigh.

"We can have all those things, we can be careful." He says, his eyes searching mine for what I'm feeling.

"How can you be so sure?" I say looking down at my hands.

"You'll just have to trust me." He puts his hand on my chin, and makes me look back at him. "Can you trust me?"

"I can try, and I'm willing to." He doesn't respond with words, instead he crashes his lips to mine. His hand moves from my chin to my cheek. When he pulls away, he rests his forehead on mine.

"Are you willing to give us a chance?" He asks, my eyes are still closed. His forehead leaves mine, and I know he's still close. I open my eyes after a few more seconds, and our eyes lock.

"I need to learn how to trust you more, but I'm willing." I say to him. Now it's my turn to search his eyes.

"I understand," He says looking sad. "Wait, you're willing?" His eyes light up.

"I am, but the moment the trust ceases to exist we're done."

"I can work with that." He says smiling. His lips find mine again. He picks me up from the couch, and flips us. Now he's sitting on the couch, while I'm straddling him. His hands move up and down my sides. His lips leave mine, to travel to my jaw than my neck. He sucks a little, causing me to moan. He pulls away to look at me. "Are we moving too fast?"

"I mean we've already had sex, it's a little late for that isn't it? We can just take the rest of our relationship a little slower." I offer.

"I like that idea. I haven't stopped thinking about how good you taste, and I need you again, soon. I don't want to rush you into it. We still need to get to know each other better." He says smiling.

"How are we going to hide this from your boss?" I ask, my concern still strong on my mind.

"I have my ways. He can't really control or even see what I do in my 'off hours'. I was technically still on duty when you fell asleep in my arms yesterday that's how he knew where you were." He pauses, keeping his blue eyes on mine. "He has like this tracker sense when the reapers are on duty, full blooded reapers are always on duty. There aren't many half human reapers because it's so forbidden, but it does happen. We are allowed to experience our human side, but for some reason we aren't allowed to fall for full blood humans. It's all complicated. So when I am on duty, and you try to save someone like you tend to do. We have to do what we normally do. Keep yelling at each other, act like we despise each other still." I nod in understanding.

"That's going to be hard, but I think we can manage. Since I definitely want to save everyone I have a premonition about, and you are meant to reap them." He smirks.

"Are you okay if we makeout a little more? We don't have to do anything else, I just need to feel your soft lips against mine some more." He asks so politely.

"Um, absolutely." He kisses me again, and we make out for what feels like hours. I'm still straddling him. My hands are in his blonde hair, one of his hands is in my hair, while the other is holding my back.

"Ehhm." Someone clears their throat from behind us. I break the kiss and look up. Clara and Millie are standing a few feet away from the couch looking at us. I get up off Lux's lap.

"Oh, hi guys." I say awkwardly. Clara sets the bags down the island, before running over to hug me.

"You did it!" She says squealing, and tightly hugging me. I laugh. Once she lets go of me, I look over at Lux. He's rubbing the back of his neck.

"I should go." he says, pointing to the door.

"No! You have to stay." Clara says a little too excited.

"I don't want to over stay my welcome." He says, rubbing his neck again.

"Please, we insist you stay." Millie says. Lux agrees. We all sit in the living room, at first it's awkward and quiet, but Clara breaks the silence. Before we know it, we are all laughing and talking like there was no awkwardness. After an hour of talking, Lux and I decide we want to go in my room to watch a movie.

"We can watch one out here together." Clara offers. Millie nudges her arm.

"They want some more one on one time."
Millie says quietly, but I still hear her. I'm not sure
if Lux did or not. Clara's face turns a light shade of
pink which makes me laugh a little. She's not as
innocent as she's playing to be, but I think she's a
little embarrassed she didn't catch on right away.
We are going to watch a movie, but if a makeout
session happens, then it happens. They head to
their room, when we walk into mine.

"What movie do you want to watch?" I ask
while closing the door behind us. I turn to face him,
but he's right behind me. I back up against the
door, his lips collide with mine. His right hand
caresses my cheek while his left hand holds my
side. His tongue swipes my bottom lip, and our kiss
deepens. I so badly want to push him onto my bed,
rip off his clothes for frustrating me earlier. I want
to see his bare chest, his strong arms, that delicious
looking v-line, but we only just got together a
couple hours ago.

We should take this slow, but at the same
time life can be too short. I'm around people dying
a lot now, and it's made me realize you have to take
a risk, you have to live like there might not be a
tomorrow, or a next week. So like I always say, fuck
it.

I use my right hand to push not too hard on
his chest forcing him backwards towards my bed.
He hits the ottoman beside the end of my bed.

"Ow." He says, his lips still on mine. I laugh,
and turns me around with him, our lips no longer

together, my lips ache for his. He pushes me back onto my bed lightly before climbing onto top of me.

"Wait," I say. He looks at me concerned. "Do you still have the *Phantom* mask from Halloween?" I see his eyes light up for a second before they flick to a mischievous look.

"Ohh, I see. I'll be right back." He plants a kiss on my still aching lips before teleporting to who knows where. When he comes back a few minutes later, I'm still laying in the same spot patiently waiting for him. He's wearing the full costume. The formal Victorian black suit, the white ruffled shirt, a perfectly tied black bowtie, the black tailcoat, and of course the half white mask. The only difference is Lux's slightly wavy blonde hair. I can tell he tried to slick it back with water or gel, but the hint of waves are still there.

"Holy...Shit. You look so hot, but that is going to be a lot to remove." I say, which earns me a smirk in return before he leans down to kiss me. His lips don't stay on mine for long, he explores my jaw with his lips, and down my neck. I pull off the tailcoat, before carefully removing the bowtie, and slowly start unbuttoning his white ruffled shirt. I can see the impatience growing on his face, but I'm going to make him beg. I'm still on the third button of seven when he rips it open.

"Hey! I don't want you to ruin this amazing costume!" I whine.

"That's too bad, darling. I haven't stopped thinking about our time together in that janitor closet. I don't just want that again, I need it." He says gritting his teeth. His v-line is showing perfectly since now all he has on besides the mask is the suit pants. Hot damn. I can't help but bite my bottom lip. He winks at me which causes my face to heat up. It has to be tomato red right now.

I can't stop myself from leaning down to lick the lines going down to his pants. I hear him suck in a breath before groaning. I look up to see him with his head back, when he feels me looking at him, he swiftly removes my black tank top. I forgot I didn't put a bra on this morning, oh well. He grabs my right breast before taking the left one into his mouth. His tongue swirls around my nipple, just how I like. I let out a moan. I can feel him smirk against my boob. He moves his mouth to my right breast, making sure to give them equal attention. He leaves a trail of kisses down my chest, onto my stomach, to my shorts. He pulls them down, and off before doing the same to my light purple underwear. He leaves kisses on my inner thigh before sucking on the soft skin, he is definitely leaving marks.

"I have missed this sight since we put my clothes back on in that closet." He says from between my legs.

Before I have a chance to say something back, his lips wrap around my clit. He gives it a light suck, his tongue flicks it, moves up and down. I can't help but moan. He already knows what I love. I'm surprised the mask doesn't get in his way, and it's going to have my scent on it for a while unless he cleans it after this.

My hand finds his hair, I tug on it as he continues to go to town on my clit. When I orgasm, I'm too sensitive for him to keep going. I grab ahold of his black belt, and undo it. I help Lux take off his pants, and his underwear. His hard, perfectly average dick flops out. I bite my lip at the sight of it.

I motion for him to sit on my vanity chair, and when he does I sit between his legs. I take another quick glance at him, we're both smirking before I take him into my mouth. I start slow, and deep which of course causes him to moan. I quicken my pace, making sure there's enough saliva so it doesn't hurt him.

"Don't you dare make me cum. I need to feel you again." He groans. I pause, before nodding. I take him back into my mouth for a few more strokes and flicks of my tongue before getting up. I grab his hand, and he pushes me onto the bed again. Lux climbs on top of me, he gives me a quick kiss, before lining his throbbing dick up with my entrance. He carefully pushes into me. We both let out a moan before he picks up the pace, thrusting in and out. He grabs one of my boobs to play with my nipple as he keeps himself held up with his other hand. Fuck, can this man get any hotter?! How can he just so be on one arm right now? He thrusts fast and hard into me. I move my hips around the same pace as him causing him to moan. Well I'm glad he is enjoying this as much as I am.

I orgasm again, at the same time he cums. He sinks down into me, breathing deeply.

"I missed being deep inside you so much, even if it's only been a few days." Lux says, looking into my eyes. Sweat is beading on his forehead. My face warms up again. We lift my black comforter up with my sky blue blanket to get underneath it. I reach over to my bedside table for the remote, I turn on my tv.

"What should we watch?" I ask, looking over at him.

"Whatever you want. Did you finish *Scream* last night?"

"No, I fell asleep during it. I've seen it over a hundred times."

"Do you wanna restart it and watch it all together?"

"I like that idea!" I say smiling like an idiot. We spend the rest of the night, cuddling naked while enjoying the movie.

Chapter Nine

Lux left in the middle of the night, I could tell he was trying to get up without waking me but he failed. I need to go to work today, but I'm just not feeling it. It's taking me forever to get out of bed, I've snoozed my alarm three times already. I can snooze it one more time, but then I'll have to take the world's fastest shower. Maybe the shower will wake me up.

I slowly sink out of bed, and onto my feet. I turn on my big light, so I can see into my closet, I squint from how bright it is. What do I want to wear today? I look through my skirts to find a black one. I decide to wear a yellow shirt with a giant sunflower on it with the skirt. I grab my bra, and a tank top to wear under my shirt, before heading into my bathroom. I take a brief shower, before getting dressed. I brush my teeth, grab my purse and my keys. I'm out the door by six thirty. I'll get to work with around five to ten minutes to spare.

I'm hoping this week goes by fast, next week is thankfully Thanksgiving Break. The first Friday of December is the 5SOS concert, and I can't freaking wait. It's one week after Black Friday. The fangirl in me wants to explode, but I have to keep my cool until the concert. I haven't had a premonition since that man I tried to save a second time, and I'm not sure if that's a good or bad thing. I get inside the school and start setting up my desk.

"Miss Nolan, can I talk to you for a second please?" Principal Owens asks, pointing to his office.

"Yeah, of course." I say, walking over and into his office. His desk is organized, it has his name stand near the edge, but it's not hanging off. He has school sports posters all over his office, and a tall bookshelf with awards, books and other stuff he collects on it. One of the administer board members is sitting in one of the chairs opposite of Prinicpal Owens, she looks familiar but I don't remember her name.

"Please, have a seat." He says, gesturing to the open seat beside the board member. He takes his seat at his desk. I nod, and sit down. "This is Abby Linder, she's the head of the administer board for the district."

"Nice to meet you. I'm Sage." I say politely, offering out my right hand to shake hers.

"I know." She says, before turning her attention back to Prinicpal Owens. Wow, that was incredibly rude.

"Abby, she saved Mrs. Perri not too long ago." He says like he is reminding her. She nods, extending her arm out to shake my hand now. I shake it firmly and respectfully. We turn our attention back to the principal.

"Miss Nolan, we have decided we only need one secretary in the office at this time, and with Mrs. Perri doing better we don't see her retiring anytime soon. I'm very sorry, but we are going to have to let you go." What? This can't be happening right now. "It's nothing you did wrong, Miss Nolan. You're welcome to use us as a reference. We would love to help you get a job at another school." I'm fighting back tears, I take a deep breath, plaster on a fake smile.

"I understand, thank you, thank you for giving me the chance here. It's a wonderful district." I say, before turning around to gather my belongings. I clean out my desk, and take everything to my car.

Once I get in the driver seat of my car, that's when I break down. I really thought I would be there for the next five years at least, I'd become the counselor. I guess that wasn't in the cards for me. I let myself cry for a few minutes, before I wipe my tears away and then drive away. I flip off the school when I'm a good distance away, instead of going home right away I head to my mom and Grams.

When I get there, their shared car is gone. Either mom is working in the office today, or something is up that I wasn't told about. I park my car in the driveway, and walk up to the door. I try it, it's locked. They almost always lock it unless it's midday and they have the main door open.

I hold the screen door open with my butt and back while I unlock the door. I walk in, and the house smells like it normally does. It's dark, so I use the lightswitch by the door to turn the big light on. Gram's chair is empty, the tv is off. Hm, she's usually awake by now. I head towards the kitchen and peak my head in, empty.

I turn to my left to go down the hall to Gram's room. I open the door quietly in case she is still sleeping. Her bed is made perfectly. Maybe Gram's took the car. I head down to my mom's office, she should be awake and working. I open the door to find her desk empty, and her monitors off. I turn around to check her bedroom which is across the hall, also empty. Okay, now is the time to call one of them. I pull up my mom's contact when my phone starts ringing. It reads "Mom 🖤", I quickly answer it.

"Hello? Where are you guys?!" I ask, now panicking a little.

"We're at the hospital. Grams fell this morning." My mom says, calmly.

"Oh my gosh! Is she okay?!" I rush back down the hall, and out the door. I quickly lock the door behind me.

"She's getting checked out right now. I didn't want to call you while you were at work, but I figured you needed to know and you'd answer if you could." She talks like it's not a big deal, it could be a big deal.

"I'm on my way."

"Oh honey, don't leave wo-" I cut her off by hanging up. I drive ten over the speed limit to the hospital. When I get there, mom is standing in the waiting room.

"Is she back in a room?" I ask, my panicking tone still in existence.

"They are prepping her in the OR." My mom responds, her eyes are watery.

"Why?"

"She has some internal bleeding, they need to go in and stop themselves. It's a fifty-fifty risk. She insisted on going through with it. They couldn't wait until you got here, I'm sorry." My mom says, she pulls me into a tight hug. When we sit down to wait for any news I send Clara a text letting her know.

"I got let go this morning. I was at the house when you called me. I was coming over to tell you."

"Aww sweetie, I'm so sorry. They didn't deserve you." My mom attempts to reassure me. Clara ends up texting me back pretty quick. Millie and her are getting dressed to come meet us here. I show my mom the text, and she nods. I'm surprised they are up this early. Usually they don't get up closer to eight for work. It's only seven-thirty. I want to text Lux to let him know since he knows my Grams, but I also don't want to bother him if he's halfway across the country reaping someone. I'll text him, so when he gets a chance to look at his phone he'll know.

> **Me:** Hey, Gram's is in the OR. She has internal bleeding from a fall this morning. I thought you might like to know.

After hitting send, I see Clara and Millie in the corner of my eye. I get up to hug them both, my mom does the same. We thank them for coming, and go back to nerve racking quiet.

Lux: I'll be on my way as soon as I can!

I smile before putting my phone back down in my lap. This is going to be the longest wait of our lives.

It's been over two hours, we've each had three cups of bland hospital coffee. We still haven't heard anything. I'm about to get up to make a fourth cup, when a doctor comes out. His scrubs are clean.

"Nolan family." He says looking around the waiting room. All four of us stand, he gestures us to follow him. He takes us to a family consultation room. We all take a seat in a chair.

"Rena suffered a lot of internal bleeding. We were able to stop some areas, but other areas we tried to stop only bled worse. She's lost a lot of blood, and we are trying to keep an IV transfusion long enough to keep her alive to let you all say goodbye." He informs us.

"What the fuck?! You made us sit down for this, when she could die at any fucking second?!" I stand up and yell.

"Sage, now is not the time."

"There won't be a better time! What room is she in?!" I yell, he flinches but doesn't answer. "What room?!"

"206, just through the OR doors, and to the right." He says, his voice shaking. My mom, the doctor and I run to her room. I'm ahead of them, but have to stop when we get to the big doors that lead to the OR.

The doctor uses his keycard to open the big doors. I take off in a sprint to her room. I overhear the doctor tell my mom he'll give us some time by ourselves. When I walk in to her room, I see her laying there very pale.

"Grams…" I say, choking back tears, a couple slipping down my cheeks.

"Oh… Sweetie… Don't… Cry." She says weakly, and pausing between each word.. Mom rushes in, we each hold one of her hands. "I… See them…"

"Mom, who do you see?" My mom asks her.

"Our husbands…" She says, she weakly lifts her arm up and points to the end of the bed. This makes mom and I officially break.

"Grams, you can't leave me, too. Not yet." I sob into her chest, I don't put my head weight on her.

"I… I have to… I'll.." She coughs dryly. "I'll always… be with you both." The ECG machine she's connected to flatlines seconds after she takes her last breath. I try to perform CPR as the nurses and doctors rush in. They take over, and try as well. After a minute, they stop.

"Time of death is nine fifty-six." The doctor from before calls out. I collapse into my mom's arms. We both sob uncontrollably into each other's arms. The doctor tells us to take as much time as we need before him and the nurses leave.

Through my teary eyes, I see a dark figure in the corner of the room. I wipe the tears away to see Lux. He gives me a sympathetic look before he does his job. He disappears which only makes me cry harder. I could use a hug from him right now. A few minutes later, he's back in the room again, this time he used the door. He is dressed in normal clothes, similar black jeans like yesterdays and a dark blue shirt.

"I'm so sorry for your loss." Lux says, bending down to where my mom and I sit on the floor beside Gram's bed still hugging each other. He pulls us both towards him into a weird hug. We don't fight it. We sit there for a few more minutes, letting the last of our tears for the time being fall. We say goodbye to Gram's once more before we leave the room. It's going to take everything in me not to break down again in front of Clara and Millie.

I see them waiting in the same chairs we were just sitting in not even half an hour ago. They stand up when they see us and rush over. Millie hugs mom, as Clara hugs me. Mom starts crying again, causing a chain reaction. All four of us women are now crying. Lux is standing there rocking back and forth on his heels not sure what to do. After a few seconds, he comes over to hug me and Clara. We all break out of the hugs.

"I'm going to head home, I need to call the funeral home to set up a good time to have one. I also just want to lay in bed." My mom says, before giving me another hug before she leaves. I kiss her cheek before she pulls away. She leaves before we do. I sigh sadly. This is the worst day ever.

"I didn't just lose my Grams today, I lost my job." I admit to the three of them. They pull me into a group hug. "Guys, stop. If I keep crying, I'm going to get a bad headache. I also just want to go home and lay in bed." They nod.

"Hey Millie, will you take her car home? I'm just going to teleport her home so she can lay down." Lux says.

"Of course, that's not a problem." She says in response. I hand her my keys. Clara and Millie walk out of the hospital doors. I was just here yesterday morning, and the last couple days. I didn't know I'd have to come back. I frown. Lux pulls me in for a hug, and the next thing I know we are in my room.

"Do you want help changing?" He offers. I nod, I don't feel like doing anything. He helps me take my shirt off, then the tank top, then the bra before slipping on my large sleep shirt. I take off my skirt before he holds out a pair of sweatpants for me to put my legs in. He lifts my blankets for me to climb into bed. He goes to turn around after covering me up.

"Please stay..." I whisper. He turns to face me.

"Of course I will." He climbs into my bed beside me. He wraps one arm around me, and I curl up next to him. I rest my head on his chest.

"I tried to save her, even after the doctors did what they could in the OR." I say to him as I stare at my tv that is off.

"I know you did, that's how you are. Plus she was your grandmother. I know she appreciated that." He says, pulling me closer. My eyes start to tear up again.

"I didn't even get a premonition warning me. Why didn't I get one?!" I cry angrily.

"I'm not sure darling."

"This isn't fair. I didn't even get the chance to tell her about us." I sob. He relaxingly shushes me repeatedly while stroking my hair like he did the last time I had a meltdown.

"Everything is going to be okay darling. She knows we are together now, and I'm sure she's thrilled. I got you." He whispers. I fall asleep to his comforts, and from the tiredness the tears cause.

Chapter Ten

It's been a week since Grams passed.
Thanksgiving is this Thursday. It'll be the first
holiday without her. Her funeral is today, the only
two reasons I'm going are one, to show my love for
her and two, my mom needs me there. I might have
lost my Grams, but my mom lost her mom. I can't
even begin to imagine the pain she's in. I'm terrified
to lose her. Clara and Millie are also going to be
supportive, plus Clara has known her for many
years, Mille in recent years. They are getting ready,
I'm already dressed in the dress Gram's got me last
Yule, or Christmas for others. It's black and has
purple flowers on it. She'd love to see me wearing it,
and it reminds me of her so it's a good chance to
wear it even if it's sad circumstances.

I'm touching up the eyeliner and mascara
that I know will just get messed up at the funeral.
I'm going to try to stay strong during my speech.
I've spent the last week crying a lot while I've
helped my mom with planning Gram's funeral.

Clara, Millie, and I get in the car to head to
the funeral home. The closer we get, the more my
stomach ties into knots. Clara parks, we all get out
and walk quietly up to the funeral home doors. I see
a lot of family I haven't talked to in years, and I
honestly don't plan to talk to them today.

They haven't reached out to me when I've
tried to reach out to them, so I'm going to avoid

them as much as I can. We find the room where Gram's casket is, when we enter the room is filled with chairs. At the front of the room, she lies looking beautiful in the mahogany red wooden casket.

There are a bunch of flowers around her casket, and a podium just in front of some. It's also just a little to the right of her casket. My vision blurs with tears, how is this real right now? I want someone to wake me up from this horrible nightmare. I want to go back to the time I was just a little girl getting ice cream with her and gramps, or even just back to my birthday when I had dinner with her and mom.

"Let's find a seat." Clara says, gesturing to the rows of empty seats. Most people are out in the entryway still talking, waiting for others or just waiting for the service to start.

"I have to sit in the front row with mom since I'm giving a speech. You two are welcome to join us if you're okay with sitting that close."

"We will sit in whichever row you do." Millie says squeezing my arm lightly. I nod, and make my way with them following to the front row. I take a seat beside my mom, she's on the very end next to the alise on left side closer to the casket.

Clara sits beside me, and Millie next to her. I grab my mom's left hand with my right to squeeze it. She looks over at me to give me a small smile before wiping her tears with a kleenex. Everyone from the entryway start making their way into the room to find a seat. There's a least fifty people here, mostly family, but I do spot some of Gram's friends.

"If I could have everyone's attention please, we are about to get started shortly. We are going to wait just a couple more minutes in case anyone is running a little behind, but we will start the service at ten o'five." The funeral home director says to everyone in the crowd. It's ten now. My mom sighs beside me. The five minutes feel like an hour. The funeral director walks back up to the podium. "Alright, it's now ten o'five, so we are going to start. My name is Jerry, and I'm going to start by saying I'm very sorry for your loss. Before I read the eulogy, we are going to have a minute of silence to honor Rena." When he stops talking, the room stays quiet for a minute before Jerry starts talking again. He reads the eulogy mom and I spent the last few days writing.

After he gets done, he calls my mom up, but she shakes her head. She can't go up there right now, so instead he calls me to the podium. Clara rubs my shoulder, and I give her a small smile just like my moms to me earlier. I stand up and walk to the podium. Jerry moves out of the way, I sigh quietly.

"Hi, I'm Sage, Rena's granddaughter. Grams wasn't just my grandma, she was another mom to me. When my mom had to work, she was there to take care of me. She would push me on the swing, feed me treats she wasn't supposed to because they could have spoiled my dinner. Sometimes they did, and sometimes they didn't." I pause to take a deep breath and wipe some tears away. I sigh again, but not as quietly as before. "Grams was the sweetest, most caring, and amazing grandma a girl could ask for. She was my light on the darkest days, even when she was having her dark days. She knew how to cheer anyone up, even if they had just met. She will be loved forever and greatly missed." I look over at her beautiful face before smiling and stepping away from the podium.

I take my seat by my mom once again. Jerry offers my mom a chance at the podium again, but she can't. She's crying so much, I don't think she'd be able to get a word out. We all stand up to walk by the casket before it shuts for the last time.

My mom and I stand there for a few minutes, admiring her beauty, but mourning her death. We walk with our arms linked out into the hallway of the funeral home. I give her a tight hug, and she holds me tightly, too. Once everyone has gone through, we all get back into the cars we came in to head to the cemetery.

***

Today was a draining day for us all. Mom's speech at the cemetery was brief but beautiful. I'm spending the rest of the day in bed. The only times I've been out of bed was to help my mom write the eulogy and to go to the funeral.

I've been bed rotting, constantly hoping I'm just in some horrible dream that I haven't woken up from. I have my blackout curtains closed, and all the lights in my room off. The only light in my room is from the tv. I have a random movie playing, I didn't care to check, I just needed the noise so my ears wouldn't ring from the silence.

A knock at my bedroom door startles me. I don't want to speak, but when another knock comes. I just tell whoever it is to come in. I keep my back to the door. I'm laying in a ball facing the wall that my bed is against. My bed sinks beside me and someone's arms wrap around me, pulling me into them. I can tell by the arm's it's Lux.

"Clara let me inside, I didn't want to teleport in here without your permission. I tried to call and text you." He says quietly, his face right by my ear. I don't say anything. I can't bring myself to say anything right now, I'm already silently crying with the way he just wrapped me in his arms. I didn't realize how much I needed this until now. "Have you eaten anything?" I shake my head no. I can feel him frown against my cheek. I hear him sigh, but not in frustration more of worry.

"I-" I start to choke out. "I hardly ate this last week. Everytime I do I get sick." I say quietly.

"You're getting sick because you aren't giving your body enough food on your usual schedule. I can go get you some soup." He offers.

"You don't have to do that for me." I say, but instead of saying something the bed lifts from beside me. His cheek is no longer on mine, and he isn't even in my bed anymore. He returns with a bag, sometime later.

He turns on my bedside lamp. I haven't seen that much light since I got home from the cemetery. I squint my eyes and force myself to sit up. Lux hands me a warm to go bowl of chicken and dumpling soup. My favorite, Grams, used to make it for me all the time when I was sick growing up. My eyes fill with tears again, but I force them away. I've cried so much today, and I know this is a sign from her. I've never told Lux about this being my favorite soup.

"Thank you." I say, before slowly eating it. I don't want to eat too fast and make myself sick. I need to keep as much down as I can. I can't sulk forever. I know that, and tonight will be my last night. Tomorrow is a new day, and Grams would want me to be my happy self. Life is too unpredictable to cry all day. I giggle to myself, Unpredictable like the 5SOS song.

"What's so funny?" Lux asks, smiling while eating his own bowl of soup next to me.

"I just had a thought come to my mind, and it reminded me of my favorite band's songs." I say, looking over at him.

"Whose your favorite band?" He says before taking a bite.

"5 Seconds Of Summer, they've been my favorite band for over ten years now. Their music has really helped me. I'm an Ashton girl, he's the drummer. Calum plays the bass, Luke and Michael both play the guitar. They all sing, Ashton a less than the other guys. They are amazing, they're also from Australia which I think is so fucking cool!" My mood has completely flipped and I'm smiling like a mad woman but I am when it comes to those four amazing goofballs.

'What's your favorite song?"

"How can I pick?! Each song is beautiful and unique. If I had to choose my top five, in no particular order, it would be *Invisible, Close As Strangers, Everything I Didn't Say, Wrapped Around Your Finger,* and, *If You Don't Know.*"

"Wow." He says, shocked. "You really do love them, don't you?"

"Yeah, their music and goofy keek videos really helped me during the darkest parts of my life and I'm forever grateful for them and their music even if they never know anything about me." He smiles before kissing my forehead.

Chapter Eleven

It's officially the day of giving Thanks. My mom is making a turkey with mashed potatoes and gravy, green beans, and the works. She insisted Lux, Clara and Millie came to join us. My mom isn't fully back to her normal self but she's close, my uncle stayed with her for a few days after the funeral to help her out. I don't think she'll ever be exactly the way she was before Gram's died, but for it being two weeks since her passing, and a little over a week since the funeral she is doing great.

We both know Gram's would smack us lightly on the head if we cried any more over her. So instead we are celebrating Thanksgiving for her. I've had three premonitions over the last four days. I was able to save two of the three, and I've also accepted I can't save everyone, but trying is what matters. Everyone deserves a chance to live a long life.

Mom and I are currently setting the nice plates out for everyone on the table. The plates are white with pink and green flowers on them. She grabs wine glasses while I grab silverware. Once the table is set, we move the food over that we've already put onto plates and in bowls.

We place the food in the middle of the table so everyone can get the amount they want, and we can just pass it around the table. It feels weird not having Gram's here, but I know she's here with us in spirit.

"Food is ready!" Mom calls from the kitchen. The three of them rush in finding their spots at the table. They acted like they haven't eaten in days. I finally got my stomach to keep food down the night Lux brought me chicken and dumpling soup, so I'm excited for the turkey, mashed potatoes, gravy, rolls, a little bit of everything.

"Thank you, Mrs. Nolan." Lux says. Clara and Millie also thank her. My mom smiles at them before passing the food around, and she pours us each a glass of red wine.

"Are you girls excited for the concert next week?" My mom asks us before taking a bite.

"Millie and I are excited, but we know Sage it way more excited." Clara says, looking over at me grinning.

"It's going to be the best concert ever." I'm smiling like an idiot again.

"What concert?" Lux asks, looking over at me with a slight disappointed look. I'm assuming it's because I haven't told him yet.

"5 Seconds Of Summer, I'm sorry I don't know why I totally spaced off telling you." I say, worry on my voice.

"It's okay! That's your favorite band, that'll be a blast. You deserve a nice, fun night out." He says, smiling before leaning over to kiss my forehead. This earns "aww's" from all the girls at the table including my mom. We enjoy the rest of dinner, talking about upcoming plans, Millie and Clara's wedding planning, and Grams.

Everyone helps clean up the table even though mom insists they don't have to help. Once all the dishes are done, the table is cleaned off and pie is served. We head into the living room to watch a movie. Lux and I sit on the floor against the couch where Millie and Clara sit. Mom sits in her chair. We saved Grams seat opened, she's probably sitting there right now. Just like we'd want her to. Mom puts on *National Lampoon's Christmas Vacation,* our yearly tradition. She'll put the christmas tree up tomorrow, or force us to help her after the movies over which, honestly, is fine too.

Mom does end up pulling out the Christmas tree after the movie with a big grin. We all smile at her as a way of agreeing to help her. We move the little table she has by the window to an empty spot beside the entertainment center. Mom opens the box to start pulling out the three pieces that need put together to make the tree. Lux grabs them to start putting them together, while us three girls grab out the other boxes that hold the decorations for the tree. Once Lux has the three pieces together, we add the garlands and ribbons first.

Thankfully, her tree already has the lights on them so we don't have to add them. After the ribbons and garlands, we each take turns adding an ornament. We talk, laugh, and cry while decorating. Grams loved decorating the tree with mom and I. We did it exactly like we are now. After decorating,

we each hug mom, I plant a kiss on her cheek and
we head home.

• • •

Lux decides to come over after leaving my
moms instead of going wherever he goes. I should
ask him about that. Does he have a house? An
apartment? Where does he go? It's ten by the time
we change into our pajamas and lay down.

"Your mom is such a wonderful person."
Lux says, after we get the blankets on us. I'm
looking through movies.

"She is, even after life has put her through
hell and back a couple times. She deserves more
than she's gotten." I look over at him, he's already
looking at me, probably admiring me. I've caught
him doing that a lot over the last couple weeks.

"I'm sure she's happy with how her life
turned out, even if it didn't go exactly as she had
planned. She got you out of it." I smile.

"Yeah, I think she'd agree to that."

"Anyway, I hope your concert is a lot of fun
next week. If you get the chance to be one of
Ashton's groupies, I hope you take the chance." He
winks at me. I lightly hit his shoulder with mine.

"I wouldn't be one of his groupies. I'd be the
one he'd find love in, the one he'd marry, all the
things." I say, daydreaming. He lightly hits my
shoulder with his time. We both laugh.

"Hey! You have me now to think about! I want to be the one you marry. The one you have little minis of, do all the things."

"Ugh fine, you're right, but if I get the chance to kiss Ashton. I'm doing it." I laugh, pointing at him. He holds his hands up in defense.

"Hey, as you should." He says, laughing. I lean over to give a kiss on the lips. I feel him smile against my lips. When he pulls away, he doesn't break our eye contact. "Life is too short, so I'm going to tell you this now. I love you. I know we've only been going out a few weeks, but I've known you for longer, I've been drawn to you since we were fifteen." I kiss him again.

"I love you, and I still kind of hate you." I say and joke.

"Meh, that's fair." He laughs. We find a movie to fall asleep to.

Chapter Twelve

Lux is gone again when I wake up. I'm used to not walking up next to him since he starts his reaper duties early. I'm just glad he doesn't wake me when he goes. I'm brushing my teeth, and getting ready for the day when I get a premonition.

I feel the cold November air, there is fresh snow on the ground. I see a lady walking her dog. She has red hair with a black beanie on. Her coat is a dark orange. Her dog looks like a husky. I see her slip on the ice hard. Her head hits the ground really hard. The dog starts barking like crazy, but I can't tell if anyone is around her. I try to look around, but the premonition ends.

I sigh, where was that? I close my eyes and focus on the background of the premonition. I just see a bunch of dead trees behind her and the dog. I need something other than the trees to help me figure out where I need to go.

That's when I realize there's a sign behind some of the dead trees. It's the trail by the local grocery store. I grab my coat, and keys. I park at the grocery store to head for the trails when I notice a dark figure standing by some of the dead trees. When I walk past him, he appears in front of me. I gulp.

"Sage Nolan." His deep voice booms. I can't see his face, his hood covers it. He's in an outfit similar to Lux's but it's fancier. It legitimately looks like a reaper costume you'd find at a store during halloween, but more exquisite.

"Um, who's asking?" I say, nervously.

"I'm not asking. I'm getting your attention. You must not save the woman you saw in your premonition. You also must stop seeing Lux. This is the one and only warning you will receive. If I see you two together, I will end your life like I've warned before." His voice is creepy, deep, and slow.

"Why can't I save her?"

"You must stop interfering with Lux's duties."

"Oh no, I'm going to continue to save people if I can, so respectfully you can fuck right off." I say, walking around him to find the lady and her dog.

"You've been warned." He booms one last time before disappearing. I can't help but roll my eyes. I find her laying on the ice. She's not breathing, I can see Lux approaching.

"Your boss is a real douche, I see where you get it from." I say, pissed off as I kneel down beside the woman. I call an ambulance before starting CPR. I talk to the dispatcher as I do chest compressions and mouth to mouth to get her breathing again.

"Yeah he can be like that." Lux says. "Did he come talk to you again?" He's standing next to the woman's body. I look up at him still working on chest compressions.

"Obviously. He knows we've been seeing each other. He threatened to kill me again."

"Ma'am, is someone there threatening to kill you? Do I need to send officers to the location?" The dispatcher says.

"No, there's no one here trying to kill me right now." I force myself to not bust out laughing.

"Okay, paramedics will be there in a few minutes."

"Okay. I need to keep doing CPR." I say, before hanging up. I continue to attempt to get her breathing.

"Sage. Sage baby. I don't think she's coming back." Lux says.

"I need to keep trying." I say, my eyes start to fill with tears. I'm mad, and sad. I do two more sets of compressions and mouth to mouth. The paramedics still aren't here yet.

"Baby, I'm sorry but she's not coming back." Lux puts his hand on my shoulder. The paramedics finally show up a minute later. Lux is about to reap her when they try to revive her. They can't bring her back either. The paramedics don't see Lux, but he ends up reaping her. I turn around and leave. I can't save everyone. It's okay, it was just her time. It's okay. I take a few deep breaths before heading home.

⁕ ⁕

"Bitch, are you ready yet?" Clara calls from the living room, outside my door. I look at myself in the mirror one last time. I'm wearing black skinny jeans with holes in them, a *5SOS* shirt from their self-title album, and a black and red flannel tied around my waist. I'm wearing black eyeliner, mascara, and black lipstick. I look hot if I do say so myself. My mom is taking us and has the car warming up outside, so we will have to deal with a few minutes of cold when we go out to the car.

"Yes, I'm ready!" I call back, before I open the door. Clara and Millie's are similar to mine, but they are wearing different 5SOS shirts, with different color flannels around their waists. Clara's is a teal, and Millie's is a dark green.

"Let's go!" Millie says. We run out to my mom's parked car. The December air is cold, Christmas is in a few short weeks. When we get to the arena, we thank my mom. She lets us know she will be back to pick us up where she dropped us off.

We get out to then take off running, carefully avoiding any ice patches on the side walk to go inside the arena. They scan our tickets. We head down to the pit, and get behind one row of girls. We're so close to the stage, this is going to be so amazing.

When my favorite band takes the stage, the three of us, and all the people around us cheer our hearts out. They perform a couple of my favorite songs, and then some. I love all of their songs, but having a few favorites is absolutely okay. We all sing our hearts out with them. I'm definitely not going to have a voice tomorrow, but it will be one-hundred percent worth it.

After the first five songs, they bring out the large inflatable dice with six of their older songs on it. We pass it around the pit, we're having the time of our lives. When the dice lands back on the stage, Michael looks at it.

"*Wrapped Around Your Finger!*" He yells into the microphone. O.M.G. Yes!!! I look at Clara and Millie excited. Everyone in the arena cheers louder than before. As they perform the song, I swear everyone in the arena is singing along with them. I know us three are.

When the concert gets done, all four line up at the front of the stage, they all look amazing, I can't help but keep my eyes on Ashton. I see him wink in my direction, was that towards me? I'm going to do a small wave back. I do, and I see him smile in response. Oh my goodness. Ashton Irwin noticed me. Is it hot in here? After the band leaves the stage, Clara, Millie, and I head to the merch stands where we each get a shirt to remember the concert.

"We have one more surprise for you." Clara says, pulling out three lanyards with a pass connected.

"What are those?" I ask, probably the dumbest question I've ever asked.

"Backstage passes!" Clara and Millie say in unison. They didn't!

"What?! You two are the best friends I've ever had. Thank you." I say hugging them both. We head to the meet and greet. I hope I can get a picture with them. There's a decent sized line already, but we're okay with waiting. We would wait for many hours if we had to, and it would be worth it. We're in the line for thirty minutes if that before we're next. It looks like they're doing pictures and signings. Woohoo! When it's our turn I can't help, but smile. This time not like an idiot, at least I hope.

Millie and Clara let me stand by Ashton in the picture, Millie stands between Calum and Michael, and Clara stands between Michael and Luke. I'm between Luke and Ashton. They snap the first picture of us all smiling, Ashton leans down and kisses my cheek just as the other picture is taken. Oh my gosh, I might pass out. After the pictures, I look over at him blushing.

"Hi. I'm Sage Nolan." I say smiling, extending my hand for him to shake. He laughs before pulling me in for a hug.

"Hi Sage, it's nice to meet you." He smiles. I introduce myself to the rest of the guys, internally fangirling. They each give me a hug and sign my shirt. They do the same with Clara and Millie.

This has been the best day of my entire life. We say thank you and bye to the best band in the world. The workers give us each a copy of the photos. We are almost out of the venue when I start getting that concert hangover, like you need to experience it all over again.

Usually it doesn't hit until the next day, but I'm feeling it now. My mom is waiting in her car just where she said she would be. The three of us climb in. We spend the drive back to the house telling her all about the concert.

Chapter Thirteen

It's been two nights since the concert, and I'm still concert hungover. I keep looking at the picture of us girls with the band where Ashton is kissing my cheek. It's such a sweet picture, I'm adding it to a frame I bought so I can add it to my bedside table. I keep reliving the night in my head, but it's not the same as the real thing. It's snowing pretty good outside, I think we are supposed to get blizzard like conditions overnight.

Clara and Millie went out of town this morning to celebrate their dating anniversary, they're going to be gone until Wednesday. I'm stuck at home by myself. I hate being alone when it's cold and getting dark out, plus losing Grams is still on my mind. My heart is still aching. Maybe I should go over to my moms, just in case the power goes out. I can get there long before the weather picks up.

I grab my phone from beside me, fuck it's almost dead, five percent. Why didn't I have it on the charger? Oh well, mom's house isn't far.

I grab my keys and my just in case overnight bag I had packed in case I wanted to go to moms during this time Millie and Clara are gone. I throw my coat and hat on. I head out to my car, it's extremely cold out, it has to be twenty degrees out here. I get in the driver seat, and try to start my car. It tries and tries to start, but it's failing. The third time it doesn't even attempt, it's completely dead. Fuck. I don't want to be alone tonight, not in this weather.

Lux is working his reaper duties all night so I can't ask him to come over. If I start walking now, I can be there in twenty minutes, and beat the winter storm. Okay I can do this. I get out of my car locking it. I start walking on the icy sidewalk, I make sure to be careful not to slip on the patches of ice. The snow is coming down fast. I'm walking as fast as I can without almost falling.

I'm about halfway there when the weather starts to get worse, the wind is blowing harder and faster. It's slowing me down since the snow is also coming down harder and faster. Even through my gloves, my fingers are growing numb from how cold it is out here.

Through my winter coat I'm shivering like horrible. I should call someone to pick me up. I grab my phone from my purse, and remove my right glove. I call my mom, my phone now on three percent.

"Hello?" My mom answers.

"Can you come get me?" I ask her. "The weather is getting worse, and I'm walking over. My car is dead, and my phone is about to die."

"Where are y-" she gets cut off. Fuck, my phone just died. I put my right glove on, my right hand is colder than my left, I also can't feel my fingers on my right hand, and even though my left is gloved still it's starting to feel the same on my left fingers. The cold is making me sleepy. I don't know how much more I can walk, my body is aching. I'm starting to not be able to feel more of my body. I fall into the snowy ground near the park between my mom's and Clara and Millie's. The snow is glittering around me on the ground and as it falls. It's so beautiful. My fingers aren't stinging anymore. That's when I realize I've been out here too long, but it feels good, the quiet heat spreading through my arms and my legs. That's when I see her standing above me. Grams.

"Grams," I say softly. "What are you doing out here? It's too cold for to be out here. You could get hypothermia."

"Oh you sweet girl." She says. "It's okay, stop fighting. You can join your father, Gramps and I now."

"Join you? You're still here." The snow is falling on me, but I can still see her standing beautiful above me.

"Not anymore." She says. I hear a car pull up on the street next to me.

"Sage?" Someone calls out. I know the voice, but I'm feeling more sleepy. It's quiet now. Just white, everywhere. I should get back up and go to moms. I should...

Chapter Fourteen

Lux

I'm ready for my reaper shift to end. I want to go to Sage's house and snuggle up with her all night, but I have to pull the night shift tonight. Death makes everyone do one night shift a week. I just got done in Georiga, now I'm heading back to the small town in Iowa where Sage and I are from. I look down at the name of the person whose next on my list, I'm sure Sage saw a premonition and is on her way to save them now. It used to piss me off when she would do that shit, but now I love seeing her there. She has a kind heart, and I wish I knew what it was like to have one like hers. That's when I register whose name I'm looking at. No. This can't be right.

Sage Nolan: Age 25, Beaker, Iowa.
Cause of Death: Hypothermia

This has to be wrong, I can't loose her. I just got her to fall for me. I teleport there, her mom is kneeling beside her. I make myself visible to Mrs. Nolan. Her mom is crying while trying to preform CPR.

"Paramedics are on their way right now, Lux." She says, not looking at me. She's still performing compressions, and doing mouth to mouth.

"We both know she can't be saved again. I'm sorry."

"I have to try." She sounds just like her daughter did the day she tried to save that man a second time. She keeps trying. I make myself invisible to her again when I hear the ambulance approaching. Mrs. Nolan is sobbing. The paramedics load her lifeless, pale, body onto the gurney and into the ambulance. Her blonde hair looks lighter than before. I make it into the back, my presence still not known to the paramedics. Her mom is following behind the ambulance to the hospital.

"We won't call time of death till we reach the hospital." One of the paramedics says to the other. They try to save her with CPR.

At the hospital, they call time of death from back at the scene, but now where her mom can hear. Mrs. Nolan breaks down right there. She just lost her mom and her daughter not even a month apart. I can't begin to imagine how she feels. I just lost the love of my life, my dream girlfriend, the girl I was going to do all the things with.

Tears fall from my eyes as I reap her soul so she can move on from the between and go to whatever's next. Now there is really a veil between us, I'll never see or talk to her again. I hate this immortal shit. I want to be fully human.

Sage's funeral is four days later, on a Thursday. Clara and Millie came back early from their trip, they rushed back after the blizzard when they heard the news. They are both more heartbroken than ever. Sage won't be at their wedding, where she was supposed to be the maid of honor, she won't even get the chance to have a wedding herself. Mrs. Nolan hasn't stopped crying since she got here.

I'm wearing a nice black tux, Sage would have loved it. I walk up to the light brown wooden casket she's lying in. Her eyes are closed, she looks so peaceful. I wish she was just sleeping, she looks like she does when she would be fast asleep beside me. Her blonde hair is curled, and she has gorgeous light make up on. I lean down and plant one last kiss on her forehead.

"I'll love you forever and always. One day, I'll find my way to you, through the veil that now separates us." I say quietly, before walking away. I know I will never be the same again. I'm filled with anger. Death doesn't know what he has coming for him now.